RAT TEETH

OTHER YEARLING BOOKS BY PATRICIA REILLY GIFF
YOU WILL ENJOY:

THE GIFT OF THE PIRATE QUEEN

Casey, Tracy, and Company
THE GIRL WHO KNEW IT ALL
LEFT-HANDED SHORTSTOP
LOVE, FROM THE FIFTH-GRADE CELEBRITY
FOURTH-GRADE CELEBRITY
THE WINTER WORM BUSINESS

Abby Jones, Junior Detective, Mysteries
HAVE YOU SEEN HYACINTH MACAW?
LORETTA P. SWEENY, WHERE ARE YOU?

YEARLING BOOKS/YOUNG YEARLINGS/YEARLING CLASSICS are
designed especially to entertain and enlighten young people.
Patricia Reilly Giff, consultant to this series, received her
bachelor's degree from Marymount College and a master's
degree in history from St. John's University. She holds a
Professional Diploma in Reading and a Doctorate of Humane
Letters from Hofstra University. She was a teacher and reading consultant for many years, and is the author of numerous
books for young readers.

For a complete listing of all Yearling titles,
write to Dell Readers Service,
P.O. Box 1045, South Holland, IL 60473.

RAT TEETH

PATRICIA REILLY GIFF
Illustrated by LESLIE MORRILL

A Yearling Book

Published by
Dell Publishing
a division of
Bantam Doubleday Dell Publishing Group, Inc.
666 Fifth Avenue
New York, New York 10103

The trademark Yearling® is registered in the U.S. Patent and Trademark Office.

The trademark Dell® is registered in the U.S. Patent and Trademark Office.

ISBN: 0-440-47457-4

Reprinted by arrangement with Delacorte Press

Printed in the United States of America

One Previous Edition

January 1990

10 9 8

CW

with love
to my son,
Bill . . .
for 126 reasons.

RAT TEETH

Cliffie

CHAPTER 1

"Watch out," Cliffie yelled from the backseat of his mother's ten-year-old Plymouth Fury. "You're going to hit the garbage cans."

Too late.

The front wheel crashed into the garbage cans as his mother screeched to a stop in front of Aunt Ida's house.

"I told you," Cliffie muttered. From the corner of his eye he could see Amy Warren. She had just poked her long nose over the fence next door.

His mother turned around and grinned at him.

"Just a couple of crummy old garbage cans. You won't even notice another dent."

Cliffie grabbed his beat-up old suitcase by the rope that held it together. He let his mother give him a peck on the cheek, then he slid out of the car.

His mother leaned over and rolled the window down. "See you day after tomorrow," she called after him.

"Right."

"Be good in school."

He kicked a stone out of his way.

"Cliffie?"

"Don't worry."

"And remember"—his mother's voice was loud—"change your underwear."

"Good grief," he said. He darted a quick look at the fence, but for once Amy Warren was nowhere in sight.

Amy Warren was trying to drive him crazy.

It was bad enough that with teeth like his he had to be the most laughed-at kid in the United States of America.

But now he had Amy Warren too. She was sticking to him like gum on his sneakers—following him everywhere so that even the kids in school had noticed.

He marched up the driveway. Halfway to the garage he set the suitcase down and took a ball out of his pocket. He narrowed his eyes into little slits, spit on his hands, then stared at the green garage doors until he could picture Mrs. Elk, his fifth-grade teacher, sitting there, right on the handle in the middle of the door.

"Too bad, Mrs. Elk," he said, and hurled the ball at her.

Mrs. Elk screeched once and fell over backward into a pool of water. A dozen alligators, their teeth razor-sharp, were waiting for her.

"Playing ball again?" a voice asked behind him.

He looked up. Amy Warren was leaning against the fence, all set to scramble over and stick her gigantic nose into his business.

He squinted at the garage doors again and tried to picture Amy sitting there, yelling like anything.

It was no use. She had spoiled his concentration.

"I see you still have that bomb of a suitcase," she said as she boosted herself to the top of the fence.

He picked up the suitcase and headed for the side door.

Amy was right behind him. "How come you weren't in school today?"

"I was so."

"I was in your classroom this morning," she said, "and your chair was still on top of your desk. You were absent. A-B-S-E-N-T."

"I was sick," he said. He'd really been in the

principal's office because of a fight with Donny Polick. "Flu."

He took a deep breath and exhaled. "See the germs floating out all over the place? Crawly ones. Green. I just saw a bunch land right on top of you."

Amy stepped back. "That's not true, Rat-cliffe."

"You'd better close your mouth—" he began, and broke off. He opened his eyes wide.

"What's the matter?"

"Too late," he said. "The biggest germ just popped right in your mouth. It's sitting on your tongue. You'll be sick by tomorrow." He aimed the ball at the back steps and wound up. "Probably dead by the weekend."

"You're a liar, Rat-cliffe," she said, but she looked worried.

"Don't call me that." He shot the ball against the bottom step. It came back at him wide and fast. He jumped for it.

"Where'd you get a name like that anyway?" she asked.

He rubbed the ball against his shirt. "Rad," he said. "Radcliffe. Not Rat."

"Peculiar," she said. "P-U-C-U-L . . ."

He frowned at her. "It's my mother's last name. Before she got married."

"Will you teach me that?" she asked.

"What?"

"To be a star thrower." She wound up an imaginary ball and threw toward the step.

Wrong. All wrong. She looked like a little elephant. A little elephant with a big nose.

He started up the steps.

"Listen," she called after him. "The third grade is starting up a team and I've got to get on it. O-N, on it."

He didn't answer. She was probably the worst baseball player in the world.

"I'm coming to the game Saturday, Rat-cliffe," she yelled. "To get some pointers."

He leaned over the steps and stuck his teeth out at her.

She blinked and jumped back a little.

He opened the kitchen door and went inside. His father's sister, Aunt Ida, was sitting at the table. In front of her was Maizie, the rubber manikin head. Aunt Ida stopped slopping makeup on Maizie's face and swiveled around to look at him.

He caught his breath.

The front of Aunt Ida's hair was white blond, the color of ginger ale. It was worse than last week.

"Hi, Cliffie," she said. She pointed to her hair. "Not so hot, huh? I can't seem to get hair color right."

He made a gurgling sound in his throat, then

grabbed an apple out of the bowl on the counter and headed for the stairs.

She called after him, "Mr. Goodwin at the beauty school says I'm ready to give perms this week. Permanents. They make the hair curly. Kind of like your mother's, you know?"

He closed the door on Aunt Ida's voice, shoved his suitcase under the bed, and wandered over to the mirror.

His teeth were sticking out right over his lower lip. He wrinkled up his nose.

Disgusting. He looked like a vampire. Even when he closed his mouth, the ends of his two front teeth stuck out like little white tombstones. Every day they grew out a little more.

He kicked at the chair. Not one thing was the same anymore. His father used to be the vegetable man at the A & P. His mother used to be a part-time waitress at the Big Spoon. And he used to go to a terrific school in Brooklyn with his old friend Matt.

That was before his teeth started to grow like weeds, before his father finished chiropractic school, before his mother and father started to fight over everything.

He pushed open the window and crawled out on the roof. For a moment it looked as if the whole world were tilting: the sloping roof, the telephone pole, even his father's new chiropractic office tacked on the back of the house.

He closed his eyes until he was sure of his balance, then he took three running steps down the roof and grabbed onto the chimney.

It was still warm from the sun. He sank down and leaned against it. He could see Amy Warren kneeling on the grass in her backyard. She had her dog cornered against the wooden fence while she tried to make him sit up and shake hands. The dog kept yawning.

Cliffie thought about making some noises so Amy would look up.

She'd probably start to scream like anything when she saw him on the roof. His father would come running out of his office. His patient would be right in back of him, still wearing one of those white nightgown things.

Aunt Ida would be next.

And then his mother. She'd drive up in the Fury, tires screeching.

They'd beg him to come down. They'd get down on their knees.

He'd jump up on the chimney and walk around on his hands.

"Please, Cliffie," his father would yell, his glasses glinting in the sunlight. "We'll go back to the old house. End the divorce. No more living a couple

Cliffie sank down and leaned against the chimney.

of days with me and a couple of days with your mother."

"You don't have to go to school," his mother would say. "You'll never have to see Mrs. Elk again."

By the time the fire engines came, all the kids in his class would be there. Sherman Armonk, Donny Polick, Arthur Vumvas.

"Tough," they'd tell each other. "He's really tough."

Tough. That was the main thing. That's what his old friend Matt had said last year when he found out Cliffie was moving to Queens.

"Don't forget Anthony Abrusco," Matt had said, tapping him on the shoulder.

"I won't," Cliffie had answered.

And he hadn't. Anthony Abrusco was the biggest baby in the world. He had cried almost every day. He had cried all the way to spring vacation. He had even cried the day before Cliffie had left to come to the new school.

He was probably back there in Brooklyn, still crying.

"Hey."

Cliffie blinked and looked down. Amy Warren was staring up at him.

"You going to jump?" she yelled.

"Not so loud," he said. "I'm just sitting here. Trying to get some peace."

"Oh." She sounded a little disappointed.

A plane streaked across the sky, leaving a long white trail. He held his hands over his forehead and squinted up.

"If you fall off there, Rat-cliffe," Amy yelled, "you'll smash your guts on the sidewalk."

He didn't bother to answer. He leaned against the sun-warmed chimney and closed his eyes.

"Rat-cliffe," Amy yelled again.

He opened one eye.

"How do you do it?" she yelled. "Throw so good?"

"You'd never learn," he said. "It's just natural." He closed his eyes again, thinking of all the practicing he had done.

"I'll give you a dollar to teach me," she said. "A D-O-L-L-E-R."

He squinted up at the sky. After a few minutes Amy gave up. He heard her back door close.

Tomorrow was Friday. He still had another school day before the weekend. It was the worst school in the United States of America. And he had the worst teacher, Mrs. Elk. The meanest piece of work he had ever seen. You could die of thirst before she'd let you out for a drink of water. You could burst before she'd let you go to the bathroom.

The only good thing about school was baseball.

He stood up, holding on to the chimney with one hand. The backyards tilted again. He steadied himself. Amy Warren's dog was digging a big hole in the Warrens' grass.

Lucky dog. He didn't have to worry about having teeth that were growing right down his chin. He didn't have to worry about living in a bunch of houses. He didn't have to worry about anything . . . except maybe having Amy on his back all the time.

Carefully Cliffie measured the distance to the window with his eye. He took three running steps and grabbed onto the windowsill.

It was only the second week in April.

There were seventy-one days until the end of school in June. He had counted them on his mother's calendar last night.

He'd never make it. It was just too long.

CHAPTER 2

"For Pete's sake," Aunt Ida called up to him. "You'll be late for school again."

Cliffie swung his legs over the side of the bed. He was still wearing yesterday's jeans and shirt. He wondered if he could get away with wearing them today.

Aunt Ida would probably spot the smear of spaghetti sauce on the side of the shirt. He yanked it off.

He padded over to his suitcase and untied the knotted rope. He had forgotten to give his mother the wash again. He held up a wrinkled gray shirt.

It had a hole under one arm. It was a good thing he didn't raise his hand in school, he thought as he pulled it over his head.

"Cliffie," Aunt Ida shouted. "Do you know what time it is?"

"I'm coming," he shouted back. "Give me a chance."

He ran his tongue over his teeth and poked his fingers into his ears. Clean enough.

He heard Aunt Ida clump to the bottom of the stairs. "Do you want what's her name on your case again?" she shouted. "You haven't been on time in two weeks."

"Elk," he called down. "Mrs. Elk. She's always on my case anyway." He grabbed his homework and clattered down on the stairs.

"Suppose your mother finds out you're late for school every day?" Aunt Ida said. "What's she going to say? You know your mother. She's going to have a fit."

Cliffie barreled into the kitchen and slid onto the chair.

His father looked up from the book he had propped up against Maizie, the rubber manikin. "Hey, Cliffie," he said. "How are you today?"

"Rotten," Cliffie said. He looked at the cover of his father's book. A bunch of bones were drawn all over the front cover. His father was still studying up on how to be a chiropractor. He said that if people would get their back bones fixed up just right, everyone would be in a lot better shape.

"Rotten?" Aunt Ida said. "How about some pancakes? Nice and crisp." She handed him a plate. "Fix you right up."

His father peered across the table at him through his thick glasses. "Rotten? Why rotten?"

Cliffie lifted a shoulder. "When am I going to get braces anyway?"

His father pushed at his eyeglasses. "Listen, Cliffie. I have two patients now." He pulled a piece of paper out of the bones book. "Suppose I had four?" He wrote some numbers on the paper and shook his head. "No. Maybe six." He started to write again.

"How do you think Maizie looks?" Aunt Ida said. "Honey-peach blush and matching lip gloss. When I open my beauty shop someday . . ."

"Maybe eight patients," his father said. "Let's see. That would be five . . . six . . . twenty . . ."

Cliffie poured some syrup on his pancakes and stuffed a big piece in his mouth. "Tastes funny," Cliffie said. He put down his fork.

"This is it," his father said. "The magic number. As soon as I get eight patients, I'll be able to manage braces. Eight."

"You only have two," Cliffie said.

"Maybe there was a little seaweed stuff in the

bowl," Aunt Ida said. "Left over from the mud pack I was making up."

Cliffie and his father looked up. "What?" Cliffie asked.

"The pancakes. Seaweed in the pancake batter."

Cliffie looked down at his pancakes. They were a little green-looking. He pushed the plate away.

"Have a granola bar instead," Aunt Ida said.

He stood up, grabbed a package of coconut granola, and started out of the kitchen. If only it were tomorrow—Saturday—not only a baseball day, but the day his team was going to wipe out the fourth graders.

"You forgot your lunch, Cliffie," Aunt Ida called after him.

He looked back. "What is it?"

"Pot roast. Sorry. All I had."

"Good grief," he said. "You can chew that stuff forever and nothing happens."

"Take it anyway. Maybe you can trade with someone."

He didn't answer. Nobody in the whole world would trade for a pot roast sandwich.

He grabbed the lunch bag, took a quick look at the clock again, then dashed down the hall. He skidded to a stop at the front door and went back into the kitchen for his homework.

Homework was the one thing he didn't fool

"Seaweed in the pancake batter," said Aunt Ida.

around with in Mrs. Elk's class. Forget one night's homework and you wouldn't have recess for the next ten years.

Aunt Ida followed him to the front door. "Have a great day, Cliffie," she said.

He waved his hand at her halfheartedly, then rushed out the door.

"Cliffie?"

He turned.

"School won't last forever," she said.

He nodded and started up the street. He was late today. Really late. There wasn't a kid in sight. They were all goody-goodies around here anyway, just dying to get to school early and get an education.

He turned down 200th Street. Late, all right. Not a kid left in the schoolyard.

He heard the bell ring and started to run.

He didn't slow down until he hit the second floor of the school. The fourth graders had spilled out into the hall. They were talking and laughing. They probably had a sub today.

Lucky.

Gunther Reed, the fourth-grade pitcher, was winding up with an imaginary ball in the middle of the hall. He probably thought he was a star.

Cliffie barreled down the hall and bumped right into a fourth-grade girl coming out of the girls' room.

She had a mouthful of braces and bangs hanging down into her eyes.

"Hey," she gasped, trying to catch her breath.

"Watch out, metal mouth," he said. He leaned forward, closer to her, and drew back his upper lip so his teeth would stick out even farther. But she didn't jump back or blink the way Amy Warren would.

"Watch out, yourself, Rat Teeth," she answered, and headed toward her classroom.

He shoved his upper lip down over his teeth. Even the fourth graders were calling him Rat Teeth now. He felt his teeth with his tongue. They were probably still growing. Any day now he'd be able to stand on them.

He rushed into Room 212.

Inside, Mrs. Elk was yelling. Not mad yelling, just yelling.

It was probably because she had been yelling at kids for about forty years. She didn't know how to talk in a regular voice anymore.

She frowned when she saw Cliffie. "Radcliffe, you're late again."

He lowered his head a little and twitched one of his shoulders. It was the only way to act when Mrs. Elk got mad. You had to keep your mouth shut and your eyeballs down.

Mrs. Elk ran her hand through her wiry grayish hair. "Go to your seat, young man."

Cliffie started down the aisle. Someone's brown-paper-bag lunch was in the way. He hopped over it.

Everyone laughed.

He frowned, then stuck his teeth out at Donny Polick, who was laughing the loudest.

"I think you'd better do a composition for homework, Radcliffe," Mrs. Elk said, "about . . ." She paused to think. "An unusual week."

Cliffie sighed. Mrs. Elk always gave the craziest compositions.

"And that reminds me," she said to him. "I've already collected last night's homework."

He reached for the folded loose-leaf on top of his lunch bag and straightened it. He glanced down.

IDA SAMSON was written on top. HOW TO MAKE FRENCH BRAIDS. Underneath was a picture of a woman with a long string of hair down to her seat. The hair was all twisted around a long pink ribbon.

He had taken the wrong homework.

CHAPTER 3

"Well, Radcliffe?" Mrs. Elk asked.

Melissa Merrins swiveled her busybody head around to look at him. Then she turned around again. "Mrs. Elk," she said in a loud voice, "it's time for media center."

"Don't call out," Mrs. Elk said. "Line up, boys and girls."

Cliffie got to his feet, trying not to look in Mrs. Elk's direction. He got in the end of the line.

"Your homework, Radcliffe," Mrs. Elk said.

Cliffie went back to his desk and pulled out his social studies book. He started to flip through the pages.

Mrs. Elk marched out the door with the two lines behind her.

He flipped through another couple of pages.

By this time the line was out in the hall. He closed the book and began to put it back into his desk.

"Well?"

He looked up and jumped.

Mrs. Elk was standing there, hands on her hips, a sour look on her face. "I'm waiting to see you put that homework on my desk," she said. "The whole class is waiting. Even Miss Bailey in the media center is waiting. We are now two and a half minutes late."

Cliffie dove into his desk again. He shuffled some books around. "It's right here," he said. "It was here a minute ago."

He dropped a book on the floor. "I guess it's in one of these books," he said, not looking up at Mrs. Elk.

He started to flip through his social studies book again. His homework from three weeks ago was stuck between pages 118 and 119. He had looked for that in his father's house for about an hour one time.

He reached for a piece of loose-leaf in the back of the book. It looked like a page of stuff they had done the day before yesterday.

"Maybe this is it," he said, and started up the aisle toward her desk.

But Mrs. Elk was gone. He could hear her yelling at the kids out in the hall.

He threw the looseleaf page into the wastebasket and raced out the door to get in the end of the line.

In the media center he sat down at one of the back tables. He had about a half hour to figure out what he was going to say about his homework.

He turned his head to look down the nearest aisle. At the far end a pile of old books had fallen off the shelves onto the floor. They'd been there for weeks, getting dustier by the minute. It looked dark back there.

He wondered whether anyone would see him if he inched his way down the aisle.

He could sit back there on the floor for the rest of the day. He wouldn't have to do one split of work.

Miss Bailey tapped on her desk for silence, then held up a red book. "This is a terrific little book," she said, opening the cover. "It's called a thesaurus."

Cliffie slumped down in his seat.

A few minutes later Miss Bailey stopped talking

about the terrific little book and looked around. No one was paying any attention. "All right, everyone," she said. "You may choose books now."

Cliffie dove into the side aisle and sat on the floor. He picked up a book so Miss Bailey would think he was reading if she passed by.

It was a pretty messy-looking book. It had a picture of an airplane on the cover and someone had drawn a moustache on the pilot.

If he took it out she'd probably blame him for drawing the picture.

The first page looked good, though. Exciting.

Melissa Merrins stepped over him.

"Ouch," he said. "Watch where you're going!"

"Do you have to hog up the whole aisle?" she asked.

He stood up quickly.

Melissa shot down the aisle away from him.

Good, he thought. She was afraid of him.

He went up to the table and signed his book out. The rest of the class was sitting around at the tables.

That's what he was supposed to do. Instead he looked at Miss Bailey. Her head was down; she was looking at a book.

He slipped out the open library door and went down the hall.

If he decided to go to the boys' room, he'd have to pass the teachers' room.

Mrs. Elk would be sitting in there having a cup of coffee and marking papers.

Maybe he should go the other way, duck right out the front door and . . .

Mrs. Crump, the school secretary, walked by. "Young man," she said. "What are you doing hanging around out here?"

"I'm not hanging around," he said. "I have to go on a message. To the first floor. Downstairs."

She kept going. "I know the first floor is downstairs," she said over her shoulder.

He hurled himself down the stairs three at a time, then stopped to take a drink at the fountain.

From the corner of his eye he saw the third-grade class marching toward him, with a substitute teacher in the front.

The substitute wasn't paying any attention to the class. In back of her the kids were fooling around, making faces.

He could see Amy Warren at the end of the line, by herself. She looked like a real mess. Her hair was kind of stringy and her nose stuck out like someone's fist.

The substitute frowned at him. "Get back in line," she told him.

"I'm not in your line," he said, outraged. "That's a third-grade line. I'm a fifth grader."

The substitute kept going. The class followed her in a raggedy line.

He stopped for a slurp of water.

Amy Warren ducked off the line and came over to the water fountain. "I've been looking around for you, Ratty," she said.

He glared at her. "Don't you ever call me—"

"I wanted to tell you something," she said. "I think your whole trouble is your teeth."

"I'm going to punch your head in," he said.

She stepped backward and fished in her pocket. "You know Casey Valentine?" she asked, taking another step away from him. "Her teeth used to be pretty awful. Then she got braces. That's what you have to do, get braces."

He didn't answer her. He bent his head over the water fountain again.

"In the meantime," she said, "I got this for you." She held out a long tan rubber band. "Shove this over your teeth maybe. At least they won't get any worse."

Cliffie looked at the rubber band dangling in her hand. Then he turned to go down the hall.

"Listen," she said, "I'm trying to solve your problems. How about helping me with mine? Help me with the baseball. That's just what I need to make myself popular."

He turned the corner and hurried toward the stairs. It would take a lot more than baseball to make Amy Warren popular. It would take a whole new face.

He went upstairs thinking about what to tell Mrs. Elk about his homework. He ducked into the media center just as the rest of his class was lining up at the door.

CHAPTER 4

Cliffie drew back his teeth and looked in the mirror.
  Ugly.
  No wonder they called him Rat Teeth.
  He pushed his fingers over his teeth as hard as
he could. Suppose his father got only one new cus-
tomer a year.
  He wouldn't have braces for another six years. By
that time he could grow a moustache. A big bushy
one. Cover his whole mouth. He could use the brace
money to buy himself a car.
  Never mind, he told himself. It was Saturday,

baseball day. He didn't have to worry about school, or even think about Mrs. Elk and the way she had carried on yesterday. "Monday," she had screamed, "I want your homework. I want your composition. And I want you to change your ways. Shape up."

He'd worry about all that tomorrow.

This afternoon he was going to show everybody, the fourth-grade enemy team, the kids in his class, the whole world, that he was tough. He just had to.

He was going to make hit after hit, home run after home run.

Tough. The toughest kid in—

"You talking to yourself?" Aunt Ida looked in the open doorway.

Cliffie jumped.

She waved her hand. "Go right ahead. I do it myself." She flashed a grin at him. "I look in the mirror and say. 'Hey, kid. Hey, beauty. You've got to be the most intelligent, the best. Nobody around here is half as—" Her voice broke off as she continued down the hall.

After a moment Cliffie could hear her singing downstairs in the kitchen.

He turned his head a little so he could see his profile out of the corner of his eye.

He was a beast.

So was Aunt Ida. A real beast with streaky dyed blond hair.

He dragged his suitcase from under the bed and opened it. After the game he had to go back to his mother's apartment.

He pulled out his dresser drawer and dumped it upside down.

A tangle of underpants, pajamas, and ripped T-shirts landed in the suitcase.

He grabbed his books off the dresser and piled them on top.

He took a last look around to be sure he hadn't forgotten anything. The room was a mess. Junk all over the place. He kicked a couple of things into the closet, tied the rope around his suitcase, grabbed it and his baseball stuff, and headed downstairs.

"See you Monday," he shouted at Aunt Ida.

She poked her head out of the doorway. "See ya," she said. "Hope you're going to win the game."

He grinned at her. "Of course I am."

He trotted down the front steps. It was a beautiful day. Warm. Perfect baseball weather.

Next door the window opened a couple of inches. A hand snaked out and waved at him frantically. "Wait up," Amy Warren shouted. "I've got to get my sneakers on."

The window banged shut again.

Cliffie tore down the path, raced across the street, and rounded the corner.

This was going to be the most important game of the year. The most important game of his life.

And Amy Warren was going to stick her long nose right into it, drive him crazy in front of the whole world.

He looked back over his shoulder. She was nowhere in sight.

Ahead of him were some of the fourth graders. A skinny kid named J. R. Fiddle straddling his bike, and another boy with glasses, talking to the girl Cliffie had called Metal Mouth.

He ducked behind a tree and waited a few minutes until they were way ahead of him.

He didn't want anyone to spoil his concentration. He had to think about the game—the strategy he was going to use, the hits he was going to make.

At last the kids in front of him turned the corner. Over his shoulder he could see Amy Warren coming.

She was screaming at the top of her third-grade baby lungs. "Rat-cliffe, where are you? Wait up."

He dove down a driveway, climbed the fence, and trotted along 113th Avenue toward the park.

It was going to be a great day, a magnificent day.

Today it wouldn't matter that he had big yellow rhinoceros teeth. It wouldn't matter that he was the class idiot of the fifth grade.

What mattered was that he was going to win the game against the fourth graders.

"Rat-cliffe, where are you?" called Amy.

For a moment he closed his eyes. He could see everyone crowding around him. He could hear them congratulating him. Maybe they'd carry him around the field.

It was going to be incredible.

He frowned. Faintly he could still hear Amy Warren shouting on the next block. "Hold up, Ratty," she was yelling. "I'm on my way."

He started to run.

Across the street from the park was an empty house. It was rotting away. He marched up the driveway and went around to the backyard.

It was overgrown and full of weeds. He tossed the 'suitcase behind a big evergreen tree and went out to the front again.

Amy Warren was streaking down the street toward the park gates. She didn't even see him.

Arthur Vumvas was coming down the street. "What do you say, Rat Teeth? I mean Cliffie."

"Nothing." Cliffie wondered if Arthur had seen him with the suitcase. It would be terrible if anyone found out that he lived in two places at once.

Everyone would think his family was some kind of a Monopoly game.

After the divorce his father had moved in with Aunt Ida in Queens. Then he wanted Cliffie there part-time.

Then his mother moved to an apartment ten

blocks away. She said she wanted Cliffie to live with her part-time too.

No, it wasn't a Monopoly game. It was a checkers game. Back and forth. Back and forth. Ridiculous.

"Playing around in that house?" Arthur asked.

Cliffie shook his head.

"What were you—"

Cliffie stuck his teeth out over his lower lip as hard as he could. He noticed that his eyes popped a little at the same time. He wondered why.

He tried it again.

This time it didn't happen. He had to move his teeth fast, he guessed, so his whole face moved.

"What are you doing?" Arthur asked.

Cliffie scratched at his teeth with his finger. "Trying to get to the park to play ball."

He hurried ahead of Arthur into the park. He could see some of the kids in the field already. Suddenly he began to feel a little worried. Suppose he struck out.

Never.

He rushed across the field. You're tough, he told himself. Tough. "This is it," he yelled to the other kids. "This is the day the fourth grade gets clobbered."

"Let's hope so," Bobby Sanchez said.

Cliffie slipped his catcher's mask over his head. "Don't hope so. Know so." He looked around at the team. "I feel a couple of home runs coming my way."

He picked up a bat off the bench and swung it around a couple of times. As he turned, he could see Bobby Sanchez sticking out his teeth.

He made believe he didn't notice. "Gonna win," he shouted at the fourth graders on the other side of the field. "And you're going to lose."

"Right," Amy Warren said behind him. "L-O-O-S-E."

CHAPTER 5

Cliffie had been shouting all afternoon. His mouth was dry, his throat hoarse. He felt good, though. He had made a couple of hits, stolen a couple of bases.

But now the score was tied.

He glanced at the field. J. R. Fiddle was at short stop for the fourth graders. And out in left field was the kid with glasses. Walter Moles.

Walter Moles wasn't such a hot ballplayer. Anyone could see that. Instead of paying attention, he was chewing on a piece of grass or something, looking up at the trees. He had struck out about four times—every time he was up.

"You're a star, Ratty," Amy Warren yelled from the bleachers.

Cliffie looked over at her. She had ice cream smeared all over the front of her, and she was crawling up and down along the top row looking like a chocolate-covered ant.

Cliffie could see the fourth graders down in front. Metal Mouth was laughing with some kids, her braces glinting in the sunlight. He wondered if she was laughing at him.

Donny Polick started to laugh too. "That your girl-friend up there, Ratty?" he asked, pointing a bat toward Amy Warren.

Cliffie glanced up. Amy was on her hands and knees now, her rear end stuck up in the air. She was writing something on a big piece of dirty paper.

Cliffie glared at her. He wished he could make her disappear. He glared at the fourth-grade girl with braces too.

Then he turned back to the team. "We gotta win this," he shouted. He jumped up and down, feeling his sneakers hit hard on the packed earth.

"Calm down, will you, Rat Teeth?" Bobby Sanchez said. "Chill it."

"But we're into extra innings," Cliffie exploded. "This is our last chance to beat the fourth graders." He picked up his bat and headed for the plate.

He stood there for a minute, watching Gunther

Reed, the fourth-grade pitcher. Cliffie wiped one hand on his shirt.

Gunther Reed wound up and hurled the ball.

Cliffie swatted it hard and began to run.

The fourth-grade right fielder scooped it up and threw it to first, but by that time Cliffie was sliding into base.

He stood up, dusted off his pants, and began to yell. "We're gonna win this. Wait and see."

He danced back and forth at the base, shouting at the top of his lungs.

They had to beat the fourth graders. They just had to. This was their last chance.

In the bleachers Amy Warren was shouting too. "Come on, Rat-cliffe."

Arthur Vumvas came up to bat.

Cliffie stopped yelling and glanced at Gunther Reed, the fourth-grade pitcher, then over at second base.

Maybe he could steal. He'd be that much closer . . .

He shot a look at the skinny shortstop, J.R.

J.R. was watching him too.

Maybe he should stay where he was. But it was his chance, a good one.

He took off, racing toward second, head down, as fast as he could. He was flying.

Just as he began his slide, he heard the sock of

the ball as it slammed into the second baseman's mitt.

He was out. The other team was up.

Out. He couldn't believe it.

The fifth-grade team was silent as they watched him grab his catcher's mask and move to his position behind home plate.

"You were right," he heard Gunther Reed tell Walter Moles. "Just before Rat Teeth started to steal the base, he stopped yelling."

Cliffie swallowed. They were talking about him.

Walter Moles grinned. "It was scientific thinking."

As J.R. walked to the plate, Cliffie rubbed his hands on his shirt. His fault. He'd been yelling and screaming, and as soon as he stopped they knew he was going to steal.

What an idiot he was.

J.R. clunked the ball in the dirt a couple of times. If the fourth graders scored, they'd win the game.

And it would be all his fault. "Get a move on," he shouted, so he wouldn't have to think about it. "Swish, you're gonna be out."

J.R. tilted his hat and got into position. The pitcher wound up.

Cliffie watched as the ball whizzed straight through the air, straight for the bat.

Crack. The ball soared over the field, way up,

high over the back fence. A home run. End of the game.

The fourth graders went crazy, pounding each other on the back, yelling and clapping.

The rest of the fifth graders went over to shake hands with them, but Cliffie didn't even move.

He still couldn't believe he had tried to steal second. He couldn't believe that he had given the whole thing away.

He had lost the game.

He was supposed to be the best baseball player in the school, the toughest kid.

Donny Polick looked over at him. "Too bad you didn't use your head," he yelled.

Cliffie pulled off his mask. "So what?"

"You think you're so hot," Sherman Armonk shouted.

"Go soak your head," Cliffie yelled back at him.

Everyone was staring at him now. He made believe he didn't notice. He picked up his bat, the good one his Aunt Ida had given him for Christmas last year.

"Gotta go home," he said.

"Good," Sherman yelled. "Stay there."

"Wait till the next game," Cliffie said. "Without me you'd lose by a mile."

"I'd be glad to find out," Donny Polick said. "You're off the team, loud mouth."

"Go soak your head," Cliffie yelled back at him.

"Yeah," Sherman said.

Cliffie slung his bat over his shoulder. "Good," he screamed.

His eyes were watering.

Ridiculous. Ten years old with leaky eyes. He started past the rest of the kids.

"Wait up," a voice screeched behind him.

He started to run.

"Look, Rat-cliffe," Amy yelled.

He glanced back over his shoulder.

Amy was holding up the piece of dirty paper.

He stared at it.

TOO BAD
~~GOOD GOING~~, RAT-CLIFFE.

LOST
YOU ~~WONE~~ THE GAME.

STILL
YOUR ^A STARE.

Everyone else was staring too.

He turned and hurried out of the park.

CHAPTER 6

It was a long walk to his mother's apartment. He could see the Q3 bus coming along Murdock Avenue.

He reached into his pocket. Just enough money. He raced toward the bus stop and got there just as the bus lumbered by.

The driver looked at him and stepped on the gas.

"Hey," Cliffie yelled.

Crazy bus driver.

Cliffie waved his arms at the back of it as it headed

away from him. He'd like to bash the bus driver right in the mouth.

Now he'd have to walk.

So what. He had nothing to do. He'd just spend the rest of the afternoon kicking around in his mother's apartment watching television anyway.

He looked back over his shoulder. There wasn't a kid in sight. They were probably over at McDonald's by this time, munching down a pack of hamburgers or maybe some vanilla shakes.

He hoped they didn't think he cared about it.

He hoped they thought he was tough.

He was glad they didn't know he was going to be hanging around alone in his mother's apartment.

He rubbed his hands on his blue and green T-shirt. There was a jagged rip right in the middle. He wondered how it had gotten there.

His mother would have a fit.

Good.

He didn't care one bit.

He dug at the hole a little and heard the sound of it tearing. He'd like to rip the whole thing into pieces.

He took the bat off his shoulder and swung it a couple of times.

There was a telephone pole in front of his mother's apartment. He headed for it and wound up.

"Are you crazy?"

He swiveled around. It was Mrs. Furman, the woman who lived in the apartment house in back of his mother's.

"Suppose you knock the telephone pole down?" she asked.

He looked up. "I couldn't . . ." he began. Then he saw she was smiling at him.

"How's your mother?" she asked.

"Okay," Cliffie said.

"And your father?"

"He's a chiropractor now. Fixes people up like new."

"You don't look very happy," she said.

He moved from one foot to the other. "Uh, sure I . . ."

"No." She shook her head. "Try singing. It really helps. When I don't feel so hot . . . my back . . ." She broke off. "That's what I tell all the women in my bridge club. 'Sing.' You should do it too. Do it in the shower. Open your mouth right up and let it out. Sing something powerful. Something—"

"Listen," he said. "I've really got to get home now."

"Right," she said. "That reminds me, one of the teachers in your school, Eleanora Elk . . ."

Cliffie took a step away from her.

"We grew up together. If you get to see her, say hello."

Cliffie ducked his head up and down. Mrs. Furman was really a loony bird.

"Don't forget to sing," she said. "It'll make you feel better. More alive, less worried."

Cliffie nodded again. He headed for his mother's apartment house and trudged upstairs.

He had forgotten his key. He stood there, hand on the bell, waiting.

Then he remembered. His key was taped to his suitcase. And the suitcase was sitting in the back of the empty house waiting for him.

The door opened and his mother poked her head out. "Is that you ringing the bell like that?"

"Never mind," he said. "I'll be back in a little while."

Fifteen minutes later, out of breath, he stopped at the corner of 205th Street. He leaned his head around a pile of bushes to make sure none of the kids in his class had come back to the park.

A couple of old men were sitting at the checkers table, and Amy Warren was pumping a swing so hard it looked as if the swing were going to sail across the park and out the gate.

He rushed down the street and stopped in front of the empty house. Next door a woman was shaking out a mat. A cloud of dusty white lint was flying around in the air. It was making her cough.

He thought about walking up the driveway to get

his suitcase, but figured he'd better wait until she was back in the house. He leaned against a tree and made chittering noises at the squirrel who was running along the overhead wires.

He kept watching the woman out of the corner of his eye.

It looked as if she were watching him too.

He glanced up at the empty house.

It was a mess. Most of the paint was peeling off the door and some of the bricks were missing from the steps.

He'd like to open one of the windows and climb inside. He'd bring a television set with him and a huge bag of food. Doritos and Yankee Doodles.

He'd stay there until school was over.

He wouldn't have to look at the kids on Monday morning.

Everybody would forget he had lost the game. They'd think he had been kidnapped or something.

Finally the woman stopped shaking her mat all over the place. She stared at him for a moment, then went inside and closed the door.

He waited another minute, just in case she popped her head out again, then he hurried up the driveway to the back yard.

His suitcase was still there behind the tree, half hidden in the tall grass. He picked it up and started for the driveway.

In back of him there was a noise. He stopped and looked around. Then he heard it again. It was a cat, meowing.

He looked up. A skinny red cat was sitting on a windowsill inside the house.

He went over to the window and, shading his eyes, peered inside. Behind the cat the room was empty.

The cat meowed again and began to scratch at the window.

"How'd you get in there?" Cliffie asked. He pushed at the window, but he couldn't get it to budge.

He had to get in somehow.

He walked around the back of the house. A heavy board was nailed to the kitchen door.

Next to the door was a small window. He shoved it up a little, and stuck his head in the opening. The air smelled musty inside.

"Here, kitty, kitty," he yelled.

Next door a window opened. "Hey," the woman yelled. "I thought I saw you going back there. Want to get hurt? Want to get in trouble?"

"It's a cat," he began, "stuck . . ."

"Get out of there right away."

Cliffie wanted to tell her to soak her head but he was afraid she'd call the police.

"Here, kitty, kitty," he whispered.

Cliffie pushed at the window.

"Did you hear me?" the woman yelled.

"I'm going," Cliffie muttered. "Keep your shirt on, will you?"

The cat jumped up on the windowsill and poked a paw out at him. It was still meowing.

"Come on, cat," he said. He reached in, pulled it out, and shut the window.

The woman was still there, her head hanging out the window like a balloon. She watched him as he picked up his suitcase again, gave the cat a pat, and trudged up the driveway.

The cat followed him.

At the front of the house Cliffie stopped to look at the cat. There was a spot of grease on its forehead and its red fur was matted and dirty-looking.

Maybe it wasn't lost. Maybe it didn't belong to anyone. Maybe it was starving.

Cliffie reached into his pocket to see if he had something to eat, but he didn't find anything.

The cat padded over and rubbed against his jeans.

Cliffie picked it up and started down the street. But the cat didn't want to be held. It jumped out of Cliffie's arms and sat on the sidewalk, licking a front paw.

"Bye, cat," Cliffie said.

By the time he reached the corner, the cat had finished washing and came after him. All the way home, he kept looking back. The cat was still there.

When he reached his mother's apartment house, Cliffie sat down on the steps. He bent over to pet the cat.

It was really filthy.

Maybe he'd better bring it inside. Maybe he'd better give it something to drink, something to eat.

He picked the cat up again and unlocked the door.

Upstairs his mother was in her bedroom, typing. The door was open. He hurried past and went into the kitchen, dumping the cat on top of the counter.

"Just a minute," he said, "milk coming up." He pulled the container out of the refrigerator.

"Cliffie," his mother said, "get that cat off there."

He jumped.

"Where did you get that cat?"

"It's mine."

She shook her head. "Uh, uh."

He didn't answer. He poured a little milk into a teacup.

"No, you don't," his mother said, grabbing the cup. She handed him a small plastic dish. "If you don't mind . . ."

He poured the milk into the dish and set it on the floor for the cat. "See," he said, "he's starving."

"Where'd you find it?"

He looked up at his mother, biting at his lower lip. "He's mine."

"You said that already."

"Aunt Ida's dying for a cat," he lied. "It's for her birthday."

His mother sighed. "You can't keep a cat. How can you take a cat back and forth?"

He reached into the refrigerator again. "It's all right for me to go back and forth, though." He pulled out a container of orange juice. "How come I can't live in one place? How come we didn't stay in Brooklyn? You and me? I could have stayed in my old school last year. I could have—"

His mother sighed again. "Do we have to go through that? Listen, Cliffie, that apartment was too big for just the two of us. Besides, your father was dying to become a chiropractor. We couldn't afford to keep it."

Cliffie poured the orange juice to the top of the glass and leaned over to slurp some of it up.

His mother wiped up a couple of drops from the counter. "And I wanted to go to school. I don't want to be a waitress for the rest of my life. I want to go to night classes, become a bank teller—"

"I could stay here at night while you're at school," he broke in.

"Until eleven o'clock? Don't be silly. You'd be roaming the streets . . ."

"What's silly is the whole divorce."

His mother shook her head. "Now I'm not going through that again. Things change. People change.

Your father and I can't say two words to each other anymore without having an argument."

She put her hand out and touched one of the cat's ears. "What's his name?" she asked.

"Anthony," Cliffie said. "Anthony Abrusco."

CHAPTER 7

"Listen, Anthony," Cliffie said on Sunday night. "I hope you didn't mind staying in all day."

Anthony didn't move. He was curled up on the windowsill asleep.

"You'd never find this place again," Cliffie went on. "Besides, tomorrow we have to move again. We've got to go to Aunt Ida's."

He felt his teeth to see if they were sticking out any farther since last night. "You belong to a traveling family now," he told the cat. "Three days with

my mother, four days with Aunt Ida and my father."
He glared at his teeth in the mirror. "Maybe I
should ask my father about staying over there with
him and Aunt Ida full-time."

"Cliffie?"

He opened the bedroom door.

"Time for a shower. Time to get ready for school
tomorrow."

Cliffie sighed. "It's always something to do," he
said to Anthony.

He grabbed a pair of pajamas and went down the
hall to the bathroom.

The window was open. He could see Mrs. Furman in the apartment window across the way. She
was smiling and nodding her head.

Most people would think Mrs. Furman was talking to herself, but Cliffie knew she was talking to
the half-dead pot of ivy on the windowsill. Maybe
she was talking about her friend, Mrs. Eleanora Elk.

He closed the window and yanked down the
shade. He'd be half dead too, he thought, if he had
to listen to Mrs. Furman going on all the time,
telling people to sing out loud in the shower.

He reached behind the red and yellow see-
through shower curtain and turned both faucets on
full blast.

By the time he'd counted to fourteen, great clouds

of white steam were billowing out around the curtain, misting up the mirror and turning the whole bathroom into fog.

He could hardly see the sink or the toilet bowl. When he held his hand out in front of him, he could hardly see that either.

It reminded him of a movie he had been watching last week. A woman was walking down the street all by herself. In the fog. Then she heard footsteps.

Just as the killer was creeping up, ready to bam her over the head with his cane, his mother had come along and switched the channel. "Junk," she had said. "Watch something worthwhile."

Now he sank down on the edge of the tub and opened his mouth wide. "Uh oh say can you see," he sang.

His voice sounded strange. Higher than he expected. Loud.

He drew a picture of a jaguar in the steamy bathroom mirror.

It looked more like a mouse.

If only he hadn't said that stuff about the team playing without him. If only he hadn't tried to steal second.

He held up his hand and wiggled his fingers around in the steamy room. They looked like fish floating in a gray sea.

It was really getting too hot.

He stood up and turned off the hot water.

"Herring boxes," he sang, "without topses, Sandals were for Clem-en-tine."

He stopped for a minute to see if he felt better, more alive, less worried.

He didn't.

His mother pounded on the door. "What's going on in there?" she yelled. "There's steam coming out around the door. It's hot enough to peel the wallpaper right off the wall."

"Just taking a little shower," he said.

"You're going to roast yourself alive in there."

"I'm out now anyway," he said. He leaned his ear against the door. He could hear his mother start down the hall.

"Crazy," he heard her mutter. "Going to turn out just like his father if he keeps it up."

He waited another minute, then he opened the door and went into his bedroom.

Anthony Abrusco was waiting for him, meowing. Cliffie picked him up and draped him across his shoulders.

His mother followed him into the bedroom. "That reminds me," she said. "Your father left a stained-glass window here. Half finished. Little bits and pieces of glass, blue and red . . ."

Cliffie curled Anthony's tail around his neck.

Anthony was purring like crazy.

"I wouldn't care that your father was a nut about stained-glass windows," she said, "except that he never finished any of them. He must have started forty-eight windows. Wait till you see this thing." She started for the hall closet.

Cliffie wished he were a cat. He could just curl up somewhere, not have to worry about fifth-grade idiots . . .

"Look," his mother said. She was dragging a window down the hall. It was the size of Amy Warren. The bottom half wasn't finished but a big white dove took up the center. It had red and blue stripes coming out of its mouth and one large horrible purple eye.

"If he thinks he's going to leave this monstrosity here," Cliffie's mother said, "he's got another think coming. Let Ida put up with this kind of thing. Let him hang it in his chiropractic office. Scare his customers."

She placed it against the hall wall and came into the bedroom. She leaned across his unmade bed and scooped up a pair of his underpants. "Look at the holes in these things," she said. "Didn't I just buy—" She broke off. "Good grief. If your Aunt Ida sees these . . . Are they all like that?"

He put Anthony down on the windowsill. Aunt Ida didn't care about underwear. She didn't care about making beds, especially when it was almost time to go to sleep in them. She wouldn't even mind hanging the dove on the front lawn . . .

"Listen," he told his mother. "I don't think I can go to school next week. I need a note . . ."

"Look at those jeans," his mother said. "I must have been blind lately. I don't know why I haven't noticed . . ." She sat down on the bed. "Tomorrow's Monday. School." She frowned.

"You could say I have a dangerous sore throat, that even the doctor's worried."

His mother pulled the blanket off the bed and started to smooth the sheets. "I can't send you back to your father and Aunt Ida looking like a Swiss-cheese freak."

"Or maybe you could say there's a growth in my throat, suffocating me whenever I try to talk, or do work."

"We'll have to wait until next weekend. Then we'll go shopping, take ourselves to Macy's and buy some lovely new underpants, a few jeans . . ."

"Why not tomorrow?" he asked.

She tossed the blanket up in the air. It landed neatly on top of the sheets. "No. You've got to go to school. Just don't let Aunt Ida get a look at your underwear. Keep it in the suitcase."

Aunt Ida never looked at his stuff anyway. Everyone just dumped clothes in the washing machine

"I don't think I can go to school next week," Cliffie told his mother.

whenever they felt like it. Sometimes the clothes didn't get washed for days and days.

"I can't go to school," he said.

"Don't be silly," his mother said. "Of course you have to go to school. You have to study. Grow up to be somebody." Her footsteps clicked down the hall into the kitchen. "Take that horror of a parrot or dove or whatever it is back to your father's when you go," she said over her shoulder.

He took a breath. He could go to Macy's. Stay there all day. Eat Chipwiches. Watch television on the big screen. If only he could get out of school.

He stood up and went into the kitchen. "Ma?"

His mother was standing at the counter eating a taco. "Want one?"

He shook his head. "Listen . . ."

"Are you going to walk around with that cat on your shoulder all day?" She licked her fingers. "Why haven't you invited anyone over here?"

"Listen," he said again. "Write me a note so I can stay home from school."

She frowned. "You can invite kids over here, you know. Just because we moved out of our house, just because this is a teensy apartment, doesn't mean that—"

"I have to have a note . . ."

His mother reached out and touched his head. "Cliffie, what's the matter?"

He twitched his shoulder and opened the refrigerator door. "There's nothing inside here. Nothing that counts," he said. "Just a bunch of junk. Butter. Ketchup . . ."

His eyes felt as if they were burning.

He was a baby, just like Anthony Abrusco. Both Anthonys.

His mother put her arms around him. "Make some friends. Invite them over."

He ducked under her arm so she wouldn't see his eyes and started for the hall.

He'd have to write his own note. Sign her name. Mail it. Say that he wouldn't be back.

In his bedroom he reached into his night table drawer for a pencil and a piece of scrap paper.

He tried to remember. Were there two *n*'s in Winifred, or only one? He thought about calling into the kitchen to ask his mother, but she'd ask him why he wanted to know.

He rested the paper on his library book.

Winifred Samson, he wrote. Winnifred Samson. One *n*.

Carefully he wrote it again. He held it out at arm's length to get a good look at it.

It was a mess.

He worked on her name for a long time, but it didn't look right. There was a little hole in one spot from erasing. He wondered why his mother had to write her name that way—a bunch of curlicues.

He crumpled up the paper and started over.

Dear Mrs. Elk,
Radcliffe Samson difinately won't be back to school this year. He has trouble with his throt. The doctor says he might have to go to the hos-pittel.

Yours truley,
Winifred Samson

P.S. I am taking him to California. Maybe the warm aire might help.

Awful. He'd never be able to put enough curlicues into the whole note to make it look like her writing.

He tapped the pencil on the paper, then stood up and went into the hall. "Ma?" he yelled. "Could I borrow your typewriter?" He opened her bedroom door and went inside.

Her voice floated back. "Don't break it. Why do you have to fool around with it anyway?"

He picked up the typewriter and bent backward to keep his balance.

It was heavy. Very heavy.

His mother came to the kitchen door as he was staggering back down the hall.

"Don't drop that," she said. "Why do you have

to carry it out of my bedroom? Why—" She broke off and went back into the kitchen.

"Don't worry," he called over his shoulder. He went into the bedroom and kicked the door shut with his foot. It would probably take the whole night to write a decent note.

He shoved a piece of paper into the typewriter.

CHAPTER 8

"Hurry up," his mother called. "You have to drop that cat and your stuff at Aunt Ida's. You'll be late for school."

Cliffie slid out of bed. Anthony Abrusco was still asleep, curled up in a lump at the foot of his bed.

Cliffie gave him a pat and threw on some jeans.

He thought about living over at Aunt Ida's full-time. He wondered if his father would say yes. He wondered if his mother would mind.

It would be strange to live away from your own mother. Kind of terrible.

He checked his pockets. He had money, every cent he had saved up. He had a token to get on the subway.

What else?

He looked around. Nothing. He raced into the kitchen and grabbed a piece of toast.

His mother smiled at him. "I have the table all set. Don't you want to—"

"No time." He raced back into his bedroom, picked up his books and his suitcase. "Let's go," he said to Anthony. He scooped him up. The cat felt warm. He had already gained a little weight. He looked great.

He hoped Aunt Ida would think so. And his father.

Ten minutes later his mother dropped him off in front of Aunt Ida's house. He struggled up the front path, glad that he hadn't bothered to bring the stained-glass window with him. He put Anthony down next to the back door. "Wait here a minute," he told the cat.

Aunt Ida was sitting at the kitchen table with his father. "I dyed my hair again," she said. "What do you think, Cliffie?"

Cliffie put his suitcase down and looked at her streaky pink hair.

"Hi, Cliffie," his father said. "Did you happen to see my stained-glass window at your mother's? I can't find it anywhere. I'll bet she has it, probably wants to keep it . . ."

"Listen," Cliffie said. "I want to ask you something." He looked at his father. "I was thinking about a cat . . ."

"A cat?" his father asked. "What about?"

"Well, how about we have one?" Cliffie watched his father's face. He could see it was going to be no. "Mom said yes. I can keep him there half the week, but the cat would be afraid if I left him there alone all the time. He needs me." He started to talk faster. "We never have a pet around here and—"

"A cat? No." His father shook his head. "Gee, I'm sorry, Cliff. We can't bother Aunt Ida with stuff like that. And the patients don't want to—"

"My birthday's next week," Aunt Ida said. "I was just asking myself what I wanted. I was trying to think of something different. Something alive maybe. Brighten up the whole place."

"Like a cat?" Cliffie asked.

"You got it," Aunt Ida said. "A nice . . ." She looked up at the ceiling.

"Red . . ." Cliffie said.

"Red cat. Right." Aunt Ida nodded. "She'd sit in the kitchen while you were in school, keep me company when I wasn't at the beauticians' school. We'd call her . . ."

"Anthony. Anthony Abrusco."

"Excellent," Aunt Ida said, grinning. "I hope she doesn't mind a boy's name."

"He."

"Better that way," Aunt Ida said. "A boy cat with a boy name. Trot him in here so I can take a look at him."

Cliffie opened the back door. Anthony was meowing on the top step. Cliffie picked him up and put him on Aunt Ida's lap.

"Listen, Ida," his father said. "A cat's what we don't need around here."

She narrowed her eyes. "Maybe that's just what we do need around here."

His father looked at Cliffie and smiled. "I'm out-voted."

"Yes," said Aunt Ida. "He has gorgeous-color fur. If I get a date, I'll wear him around my neck."

His father nodded. "That stained-glass window was almost finished. I put a purple eye in that bird. Just perfect."

"Parrots have purple eyes?" Cliffie asked.

"Parrot?" his father said, frowning. "That's a dove. A dove of peace." He closed his eyes for a moment. "Who knows what color eyes they have. It's art. You can use any color you want. Purple . . . yellow . . . pink."

Cliffie gulped.

His father took a piece of toast. "That's the trouble

with your mother too. She hasn't got any artistic talent. I hope you're not going to turn out like that."

There was a knock on the back door.

That simpleton, Amy Warren, Cliffie thought.

"I'm selling cards," Amy said, opening the door and pushing herself right in. "Birthday cards and writing paper. Stuff like that. They're spectacular. S-P-I . . . They're wild. W-I-L-D."

"How about something to eat?" Aunt Ida asked her.

Amy shook her head. "You could write to your friends in your old neighborhood, Rat-cliffe."

Cliffie glared at her, then looked down at the plastic tablecloth. There were a bunch of little plates with flowers printed on the blue background. He stuck a Rice Krispie in the middle of one of the plates. He hoped Amy wouldn't start talking about Saturday's game. He'd die if she told his father and Aunt Ida that it was his fault the fifth graders had lost.

Amy stood up. "I have to go now," she said. "I guess you don't want to walk to school with me, Rat-cliffe. We could talk about some baseball lessons for me."

"Of course he—" Aunt Ida began.

Cliffie shook his head. "No." He wiped his mouth with the back of his hand.

Amy moved toward the door. "I could wait for you outside."

Cliffie started to count Rice Krispies again. He didn't look up until he heard her close the door.

Aunt Ida shook her head. "That poor . . ."

"That elephant nose," Cliffie said.

"Shh," Aunt Ida broke in. "She'll hear you. She's standing right on the top step."

His father looked up. "Everybody has some kind of problem, Cliffie," he said. "You shouldn't make fun of Amy."

Cliffie drew his upper lip back over his teeth. "You know what my problem is," he said. "When am I going to get braces? When I'm a hundred? By that time my teeth will be falling out."

"Soon," his father said. "As soon as my practice gets going. I just started, you know. It takes time to get some patients." He smiled. "Good news, though. I got my third patient last night. Poor guy was bent over like a pretzel."

"Never mind, Cliffie," Aunt Ida said. "Right after school today, I know just what we'll do."

His father looked at the clock. "By the way, isn't it late? Aren't you supposed to be leaving for school?"

Cliffie glanced at the clock too. "I've got plenty of time," he said, thinking that the subway trains to Macy's department store left every ten minutes or so.

His father wrinkled up his forehead. "But . . ."

"Listen, Cliffie," Aunt Ida said. "It's a good thing

I'm going to beauticians' school. I've learned to analyze faces. You know, make the best of what you've
got."

Cliffie stood up. "I guess I'll go now."

"We'll do something about your hair, and your
features. After I get finished with you, you won't
even notice those teeth."

"Amy's still waiting for you," his father said.

Cliffie glanced at the window. Amy could wait for
him at the back door all day if she wanted to. He'd
go right out the front door, cut across the street,
and catch the bus to the subway.

Across the table from him Aunt Ida was frowning.
Maybe she knew what he was thinking. "What's the
matter?" he asked.

She took a sip of coffee. "Beauty school, that's
what's the matter," she said. "I'm almost ready to
graduate, start my own place, and I just can't do
color."

"Color," he repeated, his mouth full of Rice Krispies.

She waved her hands around. "You know, a lady
comes in with yuck brown hair, wants to change it
to sun gold. I can't get it right. Instead of yuck
brown, it's yuck yellow."

Aunt Ida put Anthony Abrusco on the floor and
poured him a dish of milk.

"He cries a lot," Cliffie said. "Maybe he's going

to miss me while I'm at—I mean, while I'm in school."

"Don't worry," she said. "He'll have to get used to being alone for a little while." She grinned. "We all have problems."

Cliffie looked at her anxiously. "But suppose he's worried. Suppose he thinks—"

"Don't worry," she said again. "I'm just going down to the beauty school for a little while. I'll be back early. And your father's back and forth during the day." She brushed her hands on her skirt. "I've got to go now. Don't forget about this afternoon."

"This afternoon . . ." Cliffie began.

Aunt Ida hurried down the hall. "This afternoon. We're going to study your features." Her voice floated back. "Make the best of what you've got."

CHAPTER 9

Cliffie put the airplane book and his absence note under his arm and hurried down 200th Street toward Murdock Avenue. He kept his head down and his shoulders hunched. All he needed was for someone to see him going in the opposite direction from school.

He started to run when he reached the corner. He circled around some garbage cans and tore across the street, heading for the bus stop.

He ran right into the fourth-grade girl. Metal Mouth. Her hair was hanging down in front of her eyes like Amy Warren's dog's.

"Ouch," she said. "Caught me right in the leg."

He mumbled something and kept going. He could see the bus coming along Murdock Avenue.

He looked back. She was still standing there rubbing her leg.

If she didn't get moving, she was going to see him climb right on the bus. He clenched his teeth and watched the bus getting closer.

"You're going to be late for school, Metal Mouth," he yelled, then clamped his mouth shut. He could feel his front two teeth making dents in his lower lip. He had to be the world's greatest airbrain. Instead of hurrying toward school, Metal Mouth stopped to look back at him.

Then she marched across the street.

The bus lumbered past.

"Why Metal Mouth all the time?" she asked, brushing her hair back. "Don't you have a scrap of imagination?"

He drew back his lips and stuck his teeth out at her. From the corner of his eye he could see another bus coming. It was way down on Murdock Avenue.

She began to grin. "Try something else for a change." She headed back across the street. "Something like Barbed Wire Beauty," she called. "Or Copper Choppers."

He could feel himself start to grin too. He closed his mouth.

"Tinsel Tusks." Her voice floated back.

He watched as she hurried toward school.

He waved to stop the bus as it came down the street toward him, dove in front of it, and ran around to the side door as it opened.

"Nearly got killed," the bus driver said angrily.

"I thought you wouldn't wait," Cliffie said. He dropped the fare into the box, then hurried down the aisle.

It was going to be a perfect day.

He scratched at the crayon marks on the window. Someone had written JOE & MEG 4 EVER in bright red.

He sat back and looked out the window with eyes half closed. The trees seemed blurred, and the houses ran into each other. Ferret Fangs, he thought suddenly, that's what his teeth looked like.

He'd never go back to school again. Even if Casey Valentine told Mrs. Elk she had seen him near the bus stop, Mrs. Elk might think that he was starting on his way to California. Maybe his mother had been in one of the stores on Murdock Avenue buying toothpaste for the trip. Maybe . . .

He shook his head. He'd never go back . . . well, maybe someday, if he had decent teeth . . . after he got braces . . . if he ever got braces.

He suddenly remembered the absence note. He hadn't even mailed it yet. He had to stop somewhere and pick up a stamp. He'd have to do that right away. As soon as he got to the city.

He looked up as the bus pulled into the 179th Street station. He hurried down the aisle, jumped out the door, and raced for the subway.

A train was rumbling in on the tracks below. The whole stairway was vibrating. He took the steps two at a time and jumped down the last three.

There was a woman standing in the middle of the platform. She had a bunch of packages in one hand and an umbrella in the other.

He started to race past her, but something about her looked familiar.

He skidded to a stop.

It was Mrs. Furman.

He dove behind one of the pillars and waited until she disappeared into an open train door. Then he raced to get into another car.

Behind Cliffie a pack of people pushed through the doors. They shoved him right into the middle of the car.

He tried to grab for one of the steel poles, but he couldn't reach one. He was jammed between two men who were reading newspapers. He couldn't even raise his arm to scratch his nose.

The doors closed, then the train started up. He looked over his shoulder to make doubly sure Mrs. Furman wasn't in his car, but she was nowhere in sight. Maybe she hadn't seen him.

But suppose she had? He wondered if she would

Cliffie waited until Mrs. Furman had disappeared.

call her old friend, Mrs. Eleanora Elk, and tell her
that he was playing hooky.

He looked around. There weren't any other kids
on the train.

There was a policeman, though. He was leaning
against the door.

Cliffie ducked behind someone's newspaper. Suppose the policeman managed to push through the
crowd and asked why he wasn't in school?

Desperately, Cliffie tried to think.

Maybe he could say he was visiting someone in
the hospital. His mother. He could say she had a
special kind of disease.

What disease?

Sleeping sickness. He had read about that in his
social studies book. She had been bitten by some
kind of fly. He wished he could remember the name.

He could say that he was making a quick trip into
the hospital and then he was going right back to
school. As a matter of fact, he was going to miss
only a few minutes; he went to a late school.

He could say that he was going to stay in after
three o'clock and make up his work, that he did it
a lot.

Did what? the policeman would ask.

Stayed after school. Did extra work. That he was
the smartest kid in the class. That he really believed
in a good education.

The doors opened at the Queens Plaza station and the policeman got out.

So did a couple of other people. Cliffie moved over to lean against the pole.

He hadn't realized how dangerous it was to play hooky.

He spent the rest of the trip trying to think of excuses for being in Macy's department store all by himself on a school day.

Twenty minutes later he stepped off the train and hurried upstairs to 34th Street. He stopped to buy himself a pack of bubble gum from the magazine man on the corner, then went through the revolving doors into Macy's department store.

If someone stopped him, he'd say that he needed new underwear and his sick mother had sent him into Macy's to get it.

He grinned to himself. No one would ever think a kid could make up that kind of lie.

He stayed on the escalator until he saw the floor that had all the television sets.

There were about a million, all turned on. Every one of them showed a man's face. The man was talking and smiling. Sometimes he was big. In living color. Sometimes he was little. In black and white.

Someone was sitting on the floor in front of the biggest TV set. A boy.

"Move over a little," Cliffie said.

The boy didn't move.

"Hey," Cliffie tried again. "You're hogging up the whole television set."

The boy looked up.

Cliffie could see that he was a little older. Twelve. Maybe thirteen. He had a round pig nose and little brown pig eyes.

He stared up at Cliffie for a second. "Playing hooky?"

Cliffie started to shake his head. "My mother . . . uhm . . ." He waved at the escalator. "Downstairs in the paint . . . uh . . . book department."

"Liar," the boy said, and moved over. "You'd better watch out for the security guard. You're not going to last more than ten minutes around here." He scratched at one of his ears.

Cliffie sank down and leaned against the corner of the counter. The boy's ear was filthy. All orangy.

"What's your name?" the boy asked.

"Cliffie."

"As in Clifford?"

"Radcliffe."

The boy stuck his finger in his ear again. "Fink kind of name." He pulled his finger out of his ear and looked at it. "You're going to get caught," he said.

Cliffie looked over his shoulder. There were a couple of people looking at television sets, and a woman with a grumpy-looking face was running around trying to help everyone. He shook his head. "I am not."

The boy grinned. "Said you were playing hooky, didn't I?"

Cliffie ducked his head. "You are too."

"Right. I come here a lot. I try to get into school once or twice a week. That's enough. I spend the rest of the time here, or over at Central Park."

Cliffie looked at him, surprised. He thought he was the only one who ever thought about playing hooky in a department store.

"My name's Jo-Jo Hines," the boy said, and stood up. "Time to go now."

Cliffie looked up at him. He couldn't make up his mind whether he was glad or sorry the boy was going. "Where are you going?"

The boy shrugged. "Just saw the security guard on the escalator. He'll be around here any minute."

Cliffie scrambled to his feet and looked around.

By this time the other boy was halfway across the floor. He disappeared behind the Atari counter.

Cliffie rushed over to the elevators and looked at the arrows above them.

He didn't even know what floor he was on.

He punched the up button and the down button. *Sick mother*, he told himself, *underwear. Back to school in a few minutes, don't worry, Officer.*

He looked over his shoulder. Too bad he hadn't

"My name's Jo-Jo Hines," the boy said, and stood up.

asked Jo-Jo Hines what the security guard looked like.

My teacher sent me here, to buy underwear for a poor kid in our class. He's poor. He's very poor.

Next to the elevators was a door marked EXIT.

He pushed through and started down the stairs as fast as he could.

Jo-Jo Hines was sitting on the landing at the next floor, chewing on a long string of licorice.

"Scared?" he asked when he spotted Cliffie.

Cliffie shook his head and sat down next to him. He tried to catch his breath.

Jo-Jo wiped some of the licorice off the side of his mouth.

"Hey," Cliffie said. "My book."

"What book?"

"My book and my absence note. I must have left them upstairs near the television sets."

Jo-Jo Hines pulled on the licorice string to make it even longer. "So what?" he said. "Just a book. A note. Who cares?"

"No one," Cliffie said. He tried to think of how he would get them back. He knew Miss Bailey. If he didn't send that book back to her, she'd come after him. Track him right down. Even if she had to look in California.

He stood up. "Do you think the security guard is still in the television department?"

Jo-Jo shrugged. "Probably not."

"Well, maybe I'll just go up there, take a look around. The book was pretty exciting. I was right in the middle—"

Jo-Jo stood up too. "I'm never going to read a book again." He grinned. "Haven't read one yet."

"What will you do when you grow up?" Cliffie said, then dug his teeth into his lower lip. What a dumb thing to say to a kid like Jo-Jo Hines.

"Gonna be a millionaire," Jo-Jo said. "Maybe I'll write my own book."

"Oh," Cliffie said.

"What are you going to be?" Jo-Jo asked. "Some finky kind of a thing like a teacher? With teeth like yours, you aren't going to be a TV star." He slapped at Cliffie's shoulder and started to laugh.

"I'm going to be á ball player. With the Mets." He swallowed. He probably wouldn't get any practice in for the next ten years now that he was off the team.

"All right," Jo-Jo said. "I'll go with you. Help you find your finky book." He started up the stairs. "Last one there is an ape face."

Cliffie took off after him.

Together they hit the next landing and slammed open the door.

Jo-Jo punched him in the arm and grinned. "Let's go, man."

They raced back to the television department and threaded their way through the television sets.

The grumpy-looking saleswoman spotted them. "Hey."

Cliffie looked toward the exit.

"What are you kids doing here?"

"Looking for my book," Cliffie said. "Have you seen it?"

"Haven't seen anything."

"It was about a plane," Cliffie said.

"Vroom, vroom," Jo-Jo Hines said.

"There was a pilot on the cover. With a moustache. But I didn't draw . . ."

The woman shook her head. "Try lost and found."

"But I left it right here," Cliffie said, "right in front of . . ." His voice trailed off. Maybe he hadn't left the book there at all. Maybe it was on the subway traveling around New York City all by itself . . .

"Come on," Jo-Jo said.

Cliffie could feel his heart begin to thump. "Wait a minute."

The woman walked away.

He followed her over to the counter. "Maybe someone put it underneath."

The woman started to write some numbers on a long piece of paper. "I haven't seen it," she said.

"How about I come around and look myself?" Cliffie asked. "Underneath."

"Can't do that," she said.

"I know it's here," Cliffie said, his voice rising a little. "I left it right here and I've got to have it. It's got a lot of important—"

Jo-Jo Hines yanked at his sleeve. "You're making too much noise," he said. "Everyone is looking at you. Want the security guard to—"

Cliffie shook Jo-Jo's arm off his shoulder. "Don't you see, I've got to get it back."

But Jo-Jo Hines was walking away as fast as he could.

Cliffie stared at the woman. It had taken him hours to write the absence note on the typewriter. By the time he worked up another one, it would be tomorrow or the next day.

By that time Mrs. Elk would be calling his house, trying to find out where he was.

"Please," he said to the woman, "just take a look."

The woman stopped writing. "All right." She put her pencil down and poked her head under the counter.

Cliffie spotted a man coming down the aisle, straight toward them. He was tall, heavy, with a dark blue suit.

Probably the security man, looking for kids, looking for him.

Cliffie scrunched down behind a pile of records and moved slowly to the other side of the counter.

A moment later the woman raised her head. "Where are you?"

Cliffie watched the man in the blue suit pass by. He was carrying a Macy's shopping bag. He was just an ordinary person after all.

"I'm right here," Cliffie said.

"Sorry," the woman told him. "No books. Not with a pilot, not with a plane, not with anything."

Cliffie nodded at her.

"Lost and found is on the main floor," she said. "Maybe someone turned it in."

Cliffie started for the escalator. Suppose the library book wasn't in the lost and found?

It had to be.

But suppose it wasn't?

He stepped on a crack in the escalator, feeling it become a step under his foot.

At the lost and found Jo-Jo Hines was leaning against the counter waiting for him. "Bad news," he said.

CHAPTER 10

The book was gone.

Cliffie followed Jo-Jo Hines down the aisle, trying to think of what to do next. He could feel his eyes burning again, his throat tight.

"Hey, you," someone yelled.

They swiveled around.

A woman was coming after them, moving fast.

"Come on," Jo-Jo yelled. He took off down the aisle with Cliffie right behind him.

The revolving doors looked far away.

"Grab those kids," someone yelled.

Behind him the woman was catching up. He could hear the click of her heels on the wooden floor.

Cliffie dove for the doors. Then he was outside and running. He didn't stop until he turned the corner of Seventh Avenue.

When he looked back, he couldn't see the woman anymore. He leaned against the mailbox to catch his breath.

Jo-Jo Hines was standing in a doorway grinning at him.

"We nearly got caught," Cliffie said. He swallowed, thinking he had never been so scared in his life.

Jo-Jo Hines shrugged.

"I guess they figured we were playing hooky," Cliffie said.

"Naah," he said. "It was this." He pulled a bottle out of his pocket.

"What's that?"

Jo-Jo held the bottle up in the air and squinted at it. "Some French name," he said. "I don't know."

"But what—"

Jo-Jo shook his head. "Perfume." He dumped it in the litter basket next to them. "I was just practicing. I wanted to see if I could—"

"Steal?" Cliffie asked.

Jo-Jo grinned at him. "Lift . . ."

Cliffie swiveled his head around to make sure nobody from Macy's was coming after them.

Jo-Jo punched him on the arm. "Come on, kid, let's go over to the park."

"The park?" Cliffie glanced up. The sky was gray now. It looked like rain. It was getting colder too. He wished he had worn his jacket or at least a shirt with long sleeves.

Jo-Jo punched him again. "Let's go."

"I don't know," Cliffie said, still watching the corner. "I have to get home by three o'clock."

"Plenty of time," Jo-Jo said. "It's only eleven."

Only eleven. Cliffie shivered. It seemed hours ago that he had gotten off the subway and gone into Macy's. Hours.

"You scared," Jo-Jo said, his little pig eyes half closing.

Cliffie drew himself up. "I'm the toughest kid in my school."

"Then let's go." Jo-Jo started down the street, jogging around the people who were coming out of the subway.

Cliffie followed him slowly, wondering whether he should just dodge into the subway station. He'd never see Jo-Jo Hines again anyway.

But Jo-Jo was looking back over his shoulder. "Come on, Finkcliffe, let's go."

Cliffie caught up to him. He was really cold now.

"Want to race?" Jo-Jo yelled.

Cliffie nodded. Maybe if he ran fast, he'd work

up a sweat, forget about the goose pimples that were popping out on his arms.

He pounded along in back of Jo-Jo, ducking around the people on the sidewalk.

"About twenty more blocks," Jo-Jo panted. "Then you gotta watch out for the dogs."

"Dogs?" Cliffie echoed.

"Packs of them, half wild, just waiting to tear a tough kid like you to pieces."

"You're kidding," Cliffie said. "I've been in Central Park before."

"Good," Jo-Jo said. "Then you're smart enough to watch out."

Cliffie slowed down a little. He could feel a drop or two of rain. "Starting to drizzle," he said. "Maybe we'd better think of something else."

Jo-Jo stopped at the corner. "Nothing much else to do." He wiped his nose on the sleeve of his tan shirt. "We could go over to the library on Forty-second Street, but I nearly got caught there last week." His eyes lighted up. "Or maybe we could practice some lifting. Go over to Gristede's and pick up some cake . . ."

The rain was really coming down now. Cliffie darted into a doorway. People were shooting up umbrellas all over the place. Mrs. Furman had brought her umbrella with her this morning. He wondered where she was now. He hoped she hadn't

Cliffie pounded along in back of Jo-Jo.

seen him. He hoped she wasn't on her way home to tell Mrs. Elk or his mother he'd been hanging around the subway station.

Anthony Abrusco was probably in the bedroom curled up on the windowsill. Cliffie hoped he wasn't lonesome or crying.

Jo-Jo pushed in next to him. He smelled a little like a wet dog.

Cliffie moved back as far as he could.

"How much money you got?" Jo-Jo asked. "You could lend me a little and we could get a couple of hamburgers and fries at Burger King."

"I don't know," Cliffie said a little reluctantly.

Jo-Jo nudged him. "Take a look."

Cliffie reached into his pocket and pulled out his money. One, two, three-fifty.

"That all?" Jo-Jo asked.

Cliffie patted his pocket. "Just my subway token to get home."

A fat woman came puffing up to the doorway. She had a newspaper over her head. It was dripping wet. So was her blue flowered dress. "Do you mind?" she asked. "I'm soaked."

Cliffie shook his head. He felt something pull at his hand. He looked down.

Jo-Jo had grabbed the bills and dashed out of the doorway, pushing the fat woman aside.

"Hey," Cliffie shouted. The fifty cents in dimes

and quarters dropped out of Cliffie's open hand and rolled into the street.

Jo-Jo dashed out onto Seventh Avenue and darted around the moving traffic.

"I can't believe it," the fat woman said, as they watched Jo-Jo disappear on the other side of the street.

Cliffie looked down at his hand and then toward the street. He could see a quarter lying on the sidewalk. He hurried out to pick it up.

It still wasn't enough to get him on the bus at 179th Street.

He looked around, pulling his head into his shoulders against the rain.

"Do you need money?" the woman called to him. "Come in here before you're drenched."

Cliffie raced back to the doorway. "I just need a little," he said, wiping his face. "For the bus."

The woman reached into her pocketbook and held out a bunch of change.

Cliffie took enough change for the bus from her outstretched hand. "Thanks," he said. "I really . . ."

"What's your name?" she asked.

He hesitated. Suppose she called home to see that he had gotten there all right?

"Jo-Jo," he said after a minute. "Jo-Jo Hines."

It was the only name he could think of.

CHAPTER 11

Cliffie opened the back door and let himself into the kitchen.

Anthony was sitting under the table waiting for him.

"Hi, Anthony," he said.

Anthony started to meow. He stood up and rubbed against Cliffie's legs.

"I'm home now," he said. He picked the cat up and draped him over his shoulders.

Aunt Ida came into the kitchen. She was frowning. "I've got to do something about color," she said.

"I have such a hard time with it, never comes out right . . ." She broke off. "No books?"

"Excused from homework," he said, crossing his fingers. "Got a hundred in math the other day."

"Wonderful," she said. She looked doubtful. "Since when did you start to get so good in—"

Cliffie glanced out the window. "Here comes Long Nose from next door. I'm going upstairs. Come on, Anthony."

He unwound the cat from his shoulders and cradled him in his arms. Then he raced up to his bedroom, thinking about the hundred in math. It was really true.

Everyone in the class had gotten a hundred. All they had to do was write the nine times table on a piece of paper.

Any dummy could count a bunch of nines on his fingers and write them down.

"Hi, Ms. Sampson," he heard Amy say. "How's Cliffie?"

"Fine," Aunt Ida said. "Bright as a daisy."

A chair scraped back. "I wanted to find out how he was feeling," Amy said.

Cliffie stopped dead at the bedroom door. That kid must have been in his classroom today.

He put Anthony on the floor and charged down the stairs again. "Don't say another word," he told Amy.

She stared up at him. "Hi, Cliffie."

"Shh, don't talk. You'd better get out of here now."

"Cliffie," Aunt Ida said. "I don't like . . ."

"Why can't I talk?"

"It's an experiment. For school," he said wildly. "I was in the science lab all day."

"Oh," said Amy, "I was wondering—"

"We were practicing how to communicate without talking. Like the cavemen."

"Oh," Amy said again.

"Listen," he said. "It's time for you to go now. I've got some important stuff to do."

"What important stuff?" Aunt Ida asked.

"Stuff with . . ." He tried to think. All he could remember was that he had to do something about the absence note. Fast. Before Mrs. Elk decided to call.

"Hey," Aunt Ida said. "I almost forgot. I'm going to analyze your face. Remember?"

"I could stay and help," Amy said.

"I have a lot of homework," Cliffie said.

"You just told me you were excused." Aunt Ida smiled at him. "Don't worry. I don't mind doing this. It's helpful, really. I'm learning all the time."

"What's analyzing?" Amy asked. "A-N-E-L . . ."

"Good-bye," Cliffie said.

Anthony padded into the room and meowed up at him.

"Here, kitty, kitty," Amy said. "Nice cat. Where'd you get him? Looks familiar, I think. Is he yours?"

"Yes," Cliffie said. "He's mine. M-I-N-E. Now G-O-O-D-bye."

Amy opened the back door. "I was thinking," she said, "after you get finished with your face, maybe we could play a little baseball."

He shook his head.

"Even though you lost the game," she said, "I still think you're . . ."

He turned his back on her and opened the refrigerator door. He looked at a head of lettuce until he heard the back door close. "Does that kid have to hang around here every minute?" he asked Aunt Ida.

She didn't answer. She was dragging a large suitcase into the kitchen. She opened it on the table. It was full of tubes and bottles and a big magnifying mirror with lights all around it.

She plugged the mirror into the socket. "Just take a good look at yourself."

The lights from the mirror were glaring. Cliffie blinked. Then he glanced into the mirror.

He drew his lips back.

He looked like a vampire. "Gross," he muttered.

"Not gross at all," Aunt Ida said. "But, Cliffie, do you ever run a toothbrush across those teeth? Did you ever think of trying toothpaste? I'd die before I'd let anyone see my teeth looking like that."

"I can't help it if they stick out . . ."

"Yellow," she said. "Full of gunk. Do you ever brush them?"

"Yes, this morning." He thought back. He hadn't brushed them in days. His toothbrush was hanging in the bathroom in his mother's apartment. He grinned to himself, thinking about it. When his mother saw it there this morning, she was probably ready to have a nervous breakdown wondering how he would brush.

"Besides," he said firmly. "Yellow is my natural color."

Aunt Ida squinted her eyes and looked at him. "Diamond shape," she said.

He bent down to pet Anthony. Anthony was under the table trying to eat a little piece of dust.

"Pay attention a minute, will you, Cliffie? I'm trying to tell you about your face. How to utilize your features to your best advantage."

"Yeah," he said. "Pretend I'm a rabbit and I'd look just great."

Aunt Ida grinned. "That's what I like to see, Cliffie. A little sense of humor. A little pizzazz."

She rummaged through the case and pulled out a pair of long, skinny scissors. "Speaking of pizzazz," she said, "how about I cut your hair? Give you some bangs to go with that gorgeous diamond-shaped face."

"No good," he said. "I've got some stuff to do. Do we have a typewriter around here?"

Aunt Ida snipped the scissors together a couple of times. "Come on, Cliffie. Let me give you some bangs."

He backed toward the hall door. "How about a typewriter?"

She shook her head. "Don't have one."

"I thought I saw . . ."

"It was a long time ago. The keys were missing. The whole thing was a piece of junk. What do you want a typewriter for anyway? Gonna write a book?"

Cliffie grunted. He could write a book all right. About a crazy family that lived in two houses. About a kid with teeth down to his waist. About not getting braces until he was forty years old and had a moustache.

"I think your father has another patient. Somebody called before."

He looked up. "That makes four."

"Not bad," Aunt Ida said. "Soon he'll be making a little more money."

"Yeah," Cliffie said. "Maybe I can get a brace on one tooth."

"Maybe," Aunt Ida said, and laughed.

"You could use the other tooth for a can opener," a voice said from outside on the back steps.

It was Arthur Vumvas.

"What are you doing here? How did you know where I lived?" He dug down hard on his lower lip with his teeth. He could see that Arthur was carrying his notebook.

"Mrs. Elk told me. She said—" Arthur began.

Cliffie dove out the back door. "I'll be right back," he yelled to Aunt Ida. That crazy Mrs. Elk was always sending people's homework home.

It didn't matter if you had a hundred and six fever. It didn't matter if you were dying of a stomachache.

Mrs. Eleanora Elk was in love with homework.

"Come on in the backyard," Cliffie told Arthur. He looked back over his shoulder at the door. Aunt Ida was snipping away at a little of her pink hair.

"It's your home—" Arthur said.

"Wait," Cliffie said. That's all he needed now. Aunt Ida would find out about his not being in school, then his father . . .

"Cliffie," Aunt Ida called. "Let Anthony come with you. I'm going upstairs to color my hair again."

Cliffie opened the back door.

Anthony jumped down the steps and followed them into the yard.

In the next yard Amy Warren's dog looked up from the bone he was chewing. He saw Anthony and rushed over to the fence.

Anthony spotted the dog too. His back arched and his red tail stood out straight. He streaked across the yard, up the cherry tree, and over to the garage roof.

Amy Warren's dog was frantic. He was barking, and moaning, and jumping up against the fence.

Anthony stood on the roof, crying.

Amy's back door banged open. "Stop," she screeched at the dog. "You're giving everyone a headache."

The dog didn't pay any attention.

Amy stomped out to the yard and pulled him into the house by the collar. She banged the door shut again.

"Here, kitty, kitty," Cliffie called.

But Anthony didn't pay any attention. He sat down on the edge of the roof and began to wash his paw.

"Listen," Arthur began. "About your homework . . ."

Cliffied glanced at him over his shoulder. "Tell her you couldn't find my house."

Arthur shook his head. "I can't do that. Want me to get in trouble?"

"Tell her I wasn't here, that I live at my mother's part of the time," Cliffie blurted out. "In an apartment."

"She'd never believe—" Arthur broke off. "Do you have a ladder? Maybe you could climb up and get that cat."

Cliffie went over to the garage.

Arthur followed him. He pulled a piece of paper out of his pocket. "It's math. A whole bunch of examples. Long division . . ." He grabbed an end of the ladder. "Do you really live in two places?"

For a moment Cliffie didn't answer. Maybe he should say no. Maybe he should tell Arthur to mind his own business. He thought again about asking his father to live here full-time. His mother might feel terrible.

He dragged an old step ladder out of the garage. "Yes," he said. "Two places."

"Neat," Arthur said. "Really neat. Boy, I wouldn't mind . . ."

Cliffie looked at him in surprise for a moment. Then he said, "So take the homework back. Tell her . . ."

Arthur shook his head slowly. "I'd get killed."

Cliffie leaned the ladder against the garage. "Hold this a minute, will you?" Arthur was a scaredy-cat. Panic person, he thought, remembering Casey Valentine. He stood on the third step from the bottom and reached out for Anthony.

Anthony climbed into his outstretched arms, raking him with sharp claws.

"Yeow," Cliffie said.

"I guess he's scared," Arthur said.

Cliffie jumped off the ladder and put Anthony down in the grass.

"That your cat?" Arthur asked.

Cliffie nodded. "Anthony Abrusco."

Arthur bent down and looked at the cat. "Looks like Walter Moles's cat, Carrots." He scratched Anthony's ear. "Walter's cat is lost."

Cliffie picked up the cat again. "Walter Moles? That kid in the fourth grade? It's not his cat. This cat is Anthony."

"It sure looks like Walter's cat," Arthur said. "Wait till I tell him there's another cat around here who looks just like Carrots."

"Anthony," Cliffie said. "Anthony Abrusco."

"Listen, will you take the homework?" Arthur asked.

Cliffie shook his head. He was holding Anthony tight.

Arthur set the homework paper down on top of the garbage can and put a stone on the paper to weigh it down. "I'm going to leave it right here." He started up the driveway and turned. "How about that homework, Cliffie? Don't get me in trouble."

Cliffie wanted to shout after him, "Don't tell Walter." Instead he picked up the homework paper, crumpled it up, and threw it in the garbage.

For a moment Arthur stood there. "You think you're so tough." He turned and ran up the driveway toward the street.

Cliffie set Anthony down and backed up. "Here, Carrots," he called softly.

Inside, the phone started to ring. He scooped Anthony up and hurried in the back door. He caught it on the seventh ring.

It was a woman's voice. A familiar voice. "This is Mrs. Furman."

For a moment he sat there trying to catch his breath. His heart was pumping so loud he could hear it.

"Wrong number," he squeaked, and banged the phone down on the receiver.

Mrs. Furman. She must have seen him on the subway. She must have known he was playing hooky.

She was probably dialing her old friend Mrs. Eleanora Elk right this minute. Mrs. Eleanora in-love-with-homework Elk.

He'd be expelled. He swallowed. He wasn't going back to school anyway.

But being expelled was a lot worse than leaving on your own.

Anthony stood at the edge of the table and nuzzled at his arm.

Walter Moles was going to take Anthony away from him.

He picked Anthony up. "We're leaving," he said. "First thing in the morning."

CHAPTER 12

It was still dark when Cliffie woke the next morning. He sat up in bed and reached for the light switch. Then he rustled around in his night table drawer for a pencil and a piece of paper.

Dear Dad and Aunt Ida,
I'm going to Mom's right after school today. She said we have to go shopping. Forgot to tell you. Sorry.

Love,
Cliffie.

He looked at the note. Fine. He left it on the table, then slid his legs out from under the blankets. He just hoped Walter Moles wouldn't come to the house before school to look for his cat.

He hoped he could get out of there before Mrs. Furman decided to call again and tell on him.

If he heard the phone ring, he'd just dash out of the house with Anthony under his arm. He could run faster than Aunt Ida. He'd have a chance.

"Everything's in a bit of a mess," he told Anthony. He looked in the mirror. "Just because of a bunch of teeth. Front fangs."

He rummaged around in the closet, dragging out an old blanket and a couple of sweaters. Then he threw on a pair of jeans and a long-sleeved shirt.

Finally he was ready.

Anthony followed him downstairs to the kitchen.

Aunt Ida was sitting at the kitchen table. "Hi, toots," she said. She was frowning.

Cliffie was almost afraid to ask. "What's the matter?"

She shook her head. "I still couldn't get the right color. For Maizie's hair, you know? Whatever I do looks wrong. I'm going to fail my test."

Cliffie looked at Maizie. Her hair was purple. She looked like an Easter egg.

Aunt Ida shrugged. "It's today or never," she said.

Cliffie reached for his juice.

Aunt Ida stood up. "I've got to run. Can you get yourself breakfast?"

Cliffie nodded. "Sure. No problem."

"Your father said to say good-bye. He's working with a patient." She shook her head. "Not a new one. It's number three again."

Cliffie watched her rush around the kitchen for a moment. Then she headed for the front door.

"All right," he told Anthony. "Eat a good breakfast." He poured a bunch of dried cat food on a piece of aluminum foil and got a plastic shopping bag out of the drawer.

He went to the refrigerator and filled the bag with a container of milk, some orange juice, and half a package of doughnuts. Then he went through the closets, grabbing boxes of cat food, a box of Special K, and a package of pretzels.

It was all he could find.

It wouldn't last him very long. Maybe a couple of days. Then he'd have to figure out what else he could do.

He raced upstairs and got his suitcase, hurried down for Anthony and the shopping bag, then dashed out the front door.

Amy Warren was sitting on the bottom step waiting for him.

He shoved the suitcase back in the house.

"Running around like some kind of a maniac," she

said. "I could hear you going up and down inside from out here."

"What do you want?" he asked.

"Great news," she said. "G-R-E-A-T. Can't you tell?"

He leaned against the door and eased the shopping bag down on the step. It was heavy as lead.

"Don't I look different?" she asked.

"Not really," he said.

She flipped her head around. "Your aunt gave me a perm last night. You were upstairs someplace. I was going to call you down, but Ms. Sampson said to wait till this morning. She said I was going to knock the socks right off everybody."

Cliffie squinted his eyes. Actually, she did look better. Her nose was still gigantic. And her hair looked like a yellow Brillo pad. But she looked better. Maybe because she was smiling all over the place.

"Another thing, Cliffie," she said. "I hope I don't hurt your feelings. I don't need help with baseball after all."

"Who cares?" Cliffie said, noticing that he did feel a little hurt.

"I'm a rotten ballplayer, let's face it," she said. "But I just discovered something I'm terrific at. Spelling. S-P-E-L-L-I-N-G. And we're going to have a school spelling contest. Maybe you can help me study spelling instead."

"I just discovered something I'm terrific at," Amy said.

"Sure," he muttered. "I can just see it."

She stood up. "I mean if you ever come back. I see you're running away."

"I am not," he said. "I certainly . . ."

"It's all right." She flipped her hand at her hair. "I won't tell on you." She started down the path. "You still have to take your teeth with you," she said.

"Good grief," he said.

"Just a little joke," she said. "I'm getting so used to your teeth I don't even notice them anymore."

He waited until she had turned the corner, then he reached for the suitcase and the shopping bag, and hitched Anthony up a little higher on his shoulder.

He started for the empty house.

He was halfway there when he remembered he had forgotten to put the note on the kitchen table. He wondered how soon his father and Aunt Ida would begin to look for him. He hoped they wouldn't call the police.

He stopped to switch Anthony and his suitcase from one arm to the other. He didn't know which was heavier.

Coming across the street toward him were a bunch of kids on their way to school. He squinted, trying to see if he knew them.

He turned the corner quickly, looking over his

shoulder. A girl was hurrying down the street. She looked familiar.

Casey Valentine. She was talking to Walter Moles.

He ducked behind a pile of garbage cans until Casey and Walter had disappeared up the street. Holding Anthony tightly, Cliffie gathered up his things and started down the block.

A few minutes later he reached 195th Street. The block was quiet. No one was out.

He rushed up the driveway of the empty house, watching the house next door. The shades were down. Maybe the woman who had yelled at him on Saturday was still asleep.

He went around to the back and found the place where the window was open. He shoved it up, put Anthony and his things inside, then he grabbed onto the window and pulled himself in.

CHAPTER 13

The light was dim, but Cliffie could see he was in the dining room. The kitchen was off to his left and the living room straight ahead.

Wait till everyone found out he had run away.

Anthony began to circle around his legs, crying.

Cliffie knelt down and opened the bag with their food.

Anthony kept pushing at his hand until he tore open a box of cat food and poured some of the little tan chicken chunks on the floor. Then he took a sugar doughnut for himself and went upstairs. He wandered through the empty rooms and stopped to look out one of the front windows. He could see the street and the park below.

The park looked green and pretty in the morning sunshine. He wished he could see someone walking around, though. It seemed bare, empty without the men at the checkers table and the little kids on the swings.

Everything was quiet. Still. In school the kids would be putting their books away. Maybe they'd be talking about the baseball game and how he lost it.

There wasn't a sound in the house. It was almost as if he were alone in the whole world.

He raced downstairs. Anthony had climbed into the open suitcase. He was curled up on one of Cliffie's sweaters fast asleep.

Cliffie sank down next to him. Through the dining room window he could see the yard outside.

Maybe someone would look inside.

He got up and pulled down the shades.

There was nothing to do. He should have brought a ball with him. He could have played handball against one of the bedroom walls.

He reached into the suitcase and pulled one of the sweaters out from under Anthony. He rolled it up in a ball and lay down on the floor, using the sweater as a pillow.

"I'm glad you're here," he told the sleeping cat. His voice sounded strange. It echoed a little in the empty room.

He looked up. There was an old chandelier hanging from the ceiling, but the light bulbs were missing.

He wondered what Arthur Vumvas was doing now. Social studies maybe, or reading. He'd probably told Walter Moles about the cat. He'd be glad that Cliffie wasn't in school. He could tell Mrs. Elk that he had given him the homework.

Cliffie squinted up at the chandelier. He wondered what Walter Moles was doing. He'd probably been to Mrs. Elk's room looking for Cliffie.

That's just what he would have done.

All day Walter Moles would be waiting to go over to Aunt Ida's house. He'd be hoping that the red cat was his. Carrots.

He didn't want to think about that. He didn't want to think about school, or crumpling up the homework last night.

Cliffie turned on his side and looked at the suitcase. Anthony must have heard him move because he opened his mouth and yawned so hard that Cliffie could see his sandpapery tongue and his pale pink throat.

Cliffie reached into the suitcase and rubbed the side of the cat's neck.

Maybe Anthony wasn't Carrots.

Cliffie closed his eyes. He knew just how Walter Moles was feeling.

It was dark in the room and cold. He knew how Arthur Vumvas must have felt when he crumpled up the homework paper.

Anthony stretched and climbed out of the suitcase. He curled up next to Cliffie's chest and started to purr. After a little while Cliffie began to feel warmer. He was sleepy too. Maybe he could just sleep for a little while.

It was hard to sleep, though. Anthony kept waking up and washing his tail or his paw. Besides, if he slept now, he'd never be tired enough to sleep tonight.

He'd be in this house in the dark all night. Probably Aunt Ida would find the note. She and his father wouldn't miss him. Neither would his mother. Nobody would.

After a while he sat up and took another doughnut. Then he went upstairs.

It was much brighter up there, and now he could see old men sitting at the checkers table. Three or four little kids were playing on the slide. He watched them until their mother motioned to them and they came out of the iron gates. They were probably going home for lunch.

Cliffie felt a lump in his throat. If it weren't for

Anthony, he'd go back to school. Ask them not to expel him.

The woman next door was shaking out her rug again. And someone was rushing down the street toward the park.

Aunt Ida.

She had on jeans and a yellow jacket and a bright green kerchief tied around her head.

He watched as she dashed into the park and stopped at the checkers table. After a minute she came back across the street and said something to the woman who was shaking out the rug.

They both looked at the empty house.

Any minute Aunt Ida was going to go around to the back of the house. She'd open the window and call to him. When he didn't answer, maybe she'd climb in. Yes, that's just what she'd do. She'd climb in and ask him to come home.

And he'd be glad.

Living in two places was a lot better than living in an old empty house.

Cliffie started down the stairs.

Maybe he'd even help Amy Warren with her spelling.

He dumped his sweater back in his suitcase, closed it, and started to knot the rope around it.

He looked up.

He didn't hear anything. He ran to the window

and pulled the shade aside. No one was in the back yard.

He raced upstairs. Through the window he could see Aunt Ida hurrying down the street away from him. At the corner she stopped to look back, then she crossed the street.

He felt like opening the window and calling to her, but it was too late. After a moment she was out of sight.

Aunt Ida stopped to look back, then she crossed the street.

CHAPTER 14

Anthony was waiting for him at the bottom of the stairs. Cliffie stood there for a moment, looking down at him, wishing that Aunt Ida had found them.

Anthony started to climb up his leg.

Cliffie bent down and rubbed Anthony's ear, then he went into the dining room and finished tying up his suitcase.

"Come on, Anthony," he said. "Let's go."

He opened the window and blinked at the sunshine. The air smelled new and fresh. He hurried across the backyard and started up the block with the suitcase and shopping bag in one hand and Anthony clutched to his chest with the other. As he turned the corner, he could see Aunt Ida. She was about two blocks ahead of them.

"Hey," he shouted. "Wait up."

Aunt Ida kept going.

"Hey," he shouted a little louder.

She looked over her shoulder, then swiveled around. "Cliffie," she said. "Good grief. Where have you been? I looked in the park. I kept asking people . . ."

Cliffie tried to hurry to catch up with her, but Anthony was wriggling around trying to get down and the suitcase seemed to be coming apart.

Aunt Ida came toward him. She was talking the whole time. "I went to the beauty school." She patted the kerchief that was wrapped around her head. "You won't believe it when I tell you—" She broke off and took a breath.

Cliffie put the suitcase down and looked at the rope. The whole thing was a mess. "How did you know I was gone?" he asked.

"As soon as I finished my test, I came home. I couldn't find Anthony. I looked and then I found your note on the dresser." She shook her head. "What a mess that room is. A positive disaster."

"Found my note," he repeated. "But what—"

"Just at that minute your mother called," Aunt

Ida said. "She told me she was going to take you shopping . . ."

"Really?"

"But not this afternoon. This weekend. She said she was working late. She didn't know anything about your going to the apartment today."

"You didn't tell . . ."

"Of course not," Aunt Ida said. "She'd feel so bad. Your playing hooky, lying . . ."

Anthony jumped out of Cliffie's arms and began to play with a leaf on the sidewalk.

Cliffie lowered his head. His mouth felt dry. He never thought about anyone feeling bad—his mother, Aunt Ida, his father.

Aunt Ida bent down to help him knot the rope again. "We'll have to do something about this suitcase business," she said. "Maybe you could have double sets of underwear . . ."

"I was running away."

She looked at him, her eyes filling. "How come, Cliffie, how come?" She raised her hand in the air. "Don't tell me. I know. It's this living back and forth between your mother's apartment and my house."

She reached out and gripped his shoulders. "Your mother called me yesterday. She said she was worried about you. She said maybe you'd rather live with your dad and me full-time." She rubbed at her eyes, smearing the black mascara onto her cheeks.

"But I said I didn't think so. I said you knew that we all wished we could have you full-time. Your mother wants you. Your father. And I want you. We all need you." She smiled at him. "And Anthony too."

He stood there, looking at Aunt Ida's streaky face. "Really?" he said. "I never thought of that." He could feel a warm spot growing in his chest. "Really?" he said.

Aunt Ida laughed a little. "Really."

Cliffie scooped Anthony up in his arms. He swallowed over the lump in his throat. "I messed up a baseball game," he said. "I was yelling and carrying on. Everybody thinks I'm a loud mouth . . ." His voice trailed off. "I was trying to be tough. Trying not to let anyone know I cared about having ferret fangs . . ." He thought for a moment. "Stick-out stumps." He grinned a little. "I guess maybe I don't mind so much."

Aunt Ida clapped her hand over her mouth. "Oh, Cliffie, I forgot. Mrs. Furman called."

"I knew it," Cliffie said.

"Yes, she said she remembered what you had said about your father."

"My father?" Cliffie wrinkled his forehead.

"That he was a chiropractor."

"I guess I did. I guess . . ."

"Well, her bridge club needs a chiropractor."

Aunt Ida grinned. "Do you know how many people there are in a bridge club?"

Cliffie shook his head.

Aunt Ida held up four fingers. "Four. That makes eight patients."

"Enough for braces."

Aunt Ida nodded. "But the reason she thought about the chiropractor business was because she found your book. A library book signed out to you. In Macy's. She knew you'd be worried about it."

"It's got all my stuff in it . . ."

Aunt Ida shook her head. "No. Sorry. Mrs. Furman said there were some papers, but she dropped the book when she was crossing the street and everything fell out. The papers are gone."

"I'm going to be expelled anyway," Cliffie said.

"For playing hooky?" Aunt Ida looked at him seriously. "I'll write a note to Mrs. Elk. Say that there were some family problems." She sighed. "That's the truth. But, Cliffie . . ."

"I know," he said. "I won't do it again."

They trudged up the driveway and Aunt Ida opened the door.

Cliffie followed her inside and put Anthony down on the floor.

"Look, Cliffie," Aunt Ida said.

She unknotted her kerchief and pulled it off.

Cliffie gasped. Even with the smudges of makeup

around her eyes, Aunt Ida looked beautiful. Her hair was a soft reddish color. "Wow," he said. "It's the same color as—"

She nodded. "I passed my test. Everyone said I've invented a new color. I call it Alluring Anthony Red."

"It's exactly . . ."

"I know—the same as Anthony's." She pulled off her jacket and took out some milk for the cat. "Listen," she said, "if you guys ran away, this place would be terrible. Lonely, you know?"

"You'd still have my father."

She shook her head. "Not enough. I like having you here, and Anthony. It makes a family."

Cliffie watched Anthony lapping up the milk. "I think Anthony belongs to another family," he said after a moment. "I think he belongs to Walter Moles. I don't think his name is Anthony. I think it's Carrots. I have to bring him back."

Aunt Ida shut her eyes for a moment. She put her hand on Cliffie's arm and smiled a little. "You're one tough kid," she said.

He shook his head. "No. Anthony's the tough one. He's had a hard time, getting lost and everything." He hesitated. "Do I have to go back to school today?"

She looked at the clock. "It's almost over. Wait till tomorrow."

Cliffie picked Anthony up and went into the den. He'd have about an hour to watch television before he had to go to Walter Moles's house. He turned on a quiz show and sat on the floor to play with Anthony.

The hour went fast. At the end of the second quiz show he stood up. "I'm going now," he called in to Aunt Ida.

Aunt Ida came into the den. "How do you know where Walter Moles lives?"

"I saw him on 200th Street the other day. I'll look around there. If not, I'll ask Arthur."

Aunt Ida gave Anthony a pat. "Maybe we could get another . . ."

"Don't say that," Cliffie said. "I don't want another cat. I just want Anthony."

He bent down and picked him up. "I think Anthony may want Walter Moles, though."

He went out the back door, down the driveway, and over to 200th Street, carrying Anthony in his arms.

There were three kids sitting on the steps in front of a house halfway down the street: J. R. Fiddle, the fourth-grade shortstop; Casey Valentine, her braces glinting as she talked; and Walter Moles.

"Hey," Cliffie said. For a moment he held on to Anthony tightly. "Hey," he said again.

Walter Moles looked at him and then at the

cat. He stood up and walked down the path to Cliffie.

"He was in the empty house near the park," Cliffie said. "I found him the other day. I call him Anthony."

Walter reached out and scratched Anthony under the chin.

Casey Valentine came down the steps.

Cliffie swallowed. "Hi . . ." He hesitated. "Hi, Aluminum . . ." He tried to think of something to go with A, but all he could see was Walter Moles petting Anthony. And Anthony was purring like crazy.

"How about Dramatic Dentures," Casey said.

"Right," he said.

"Come on up and sit on the steps," Walter said. "I'll get Carrots. They're the same color, but Carrots is bigger, fatter." He looked over his shoulder. "She was lost for a couple of days, but she came back home yesterday."

Cliffie collapsed on the steps with Anthony in his arms. For a moment he couldn't say anything.

"I don't think that cat belongs to anyone," Casey said. "Some kids were feeding him in the park the other day."

Cliffie rubbed Anthony's soft fur. "He's mine now," he said. "Part of my family."

Walter came to the window and pulled the cur-

Cliffie held Anthony a little tighter.

tains aside. A fat red cat was sitting on the sill. "Can't let her out," Walter called. "You know how cats are. She might not be friendly."

"Right," Cliffie said. He held Anthony a little tighter. Wait till Aunt Ida heard . . .

"I'm getting braces," he told Casey, and stuck his teeth out.

"No more Rat Teeth," she said.

"Now I'll be Metal Mouth," Cliffie said.

Casey grinned. "Walter's grandmother is teaching me French. She calls braces *appareil*."

J. R. Fiddle tapped him on the shoulder. "Gonna play another game?"

Cliffie stood up. "I'll ask the rest of the guys. Arthur Vumvas. Donny Polick," he said slowly. "Tell them I'm sorry about Saturday."

"The fourth graders will win," J.R. said. "No doubt about it."

"We'll see." Cliffie grinned. "See you at the park. Tomorrow. Right after school."

PATRICIA REILLY GIFF

writes about girls and boys just like you:

• clever • cheerful • stubborn • mad • brainy • average • happy • sad

__THE FOURTH-GRADE CELEBRITY	42676-6	$3.25
__THE GIFT OF THE PIRATE QUEEN	43046-1	$3.25
__THE GIRL WHO KNEW IT ALL	42855-6	$3.25
__HAVE YOU SEEN HYACINTH MACAW?	43450-5	$3.25
__LEFT-HANDED SHORTSTOP	44672-4	$2.95
__LORETTA P. SWEENY, WHERE ARE YOU?	44926-X	$3.25
__LOVE, FROM THE FIFTH-GRADE CELEBRITY	44948-0	$2.75
__RAT TEETH	47457-4	$3.25
__THE WINTER WORM BUSINESS	49259-9	$2.95
__TOOTSIE TANNER, WHY DON'T YOU TALK	40239-5	$2.95
__POOPSIE POMERANTZ, PICK UP YOUR FEET	40287-5	$2.95